THE WINDY HILL

CORNELIA MEIGS

Copyright © 2015 Cornelia Meigs

All rights reserved.

ISBN: 1508955549
ISBN-13: 978-1508955542

Contents

CHAPTER I. THE BEEMAN 5

CHAPTER II. THE SEVEN BROTHERS OF THE SUN 19

CHAPTER III. JOHN MASSEY'S LANDLORD 35

CHAPTER IV. THE GARDEN WALL 49

CHAPTER V. THE GHOST SHIP 58

CHAPTER VI. JANET'S ADVENTURE 74

CHAPTER VII. THE PORTRAIT OF CICELY 85

CHAPTER VIII. THE FIDDLER OF APPLE TREE LANE 95

CHAPTER IX. THE FIDDLER OF APPLE TREE LANE *(Continued)* . 109

CHAPTER X. A MAN OF STRAW 119

CHAPTER XI. THREE COUSINS 129

CHAPTER XII. MEDFORD RIVER 145

Contents

CHAPTER I. THE BEEMAN 5

CHAPTER II. THE SEVEN BROTHERS OF THE SUN 19

CHAPTER III. JOHN MASSEY'S LANDLORD 35

CHAPTER IV. THE GARDEN WALL 49

CHAPTER V. THE GHOST SHIP 58

CHAPTER VI. JANET'S ADVENTURE 74

CHAPTER VII. THE PORTRAIT OF CICELY 85

CHAPTER VIII. THE FIDDLER OF APPLE TREE LANE 95

CHAPTER IX. THE FIDDLER OF APPLE TREE LANE *(Continued)* . *109*

CHAPTER X. A MAN OF STRAW 119

CHAPTER XI. THREE COUSINS 129

CHAPTER XII. MEDFORD RIVER 145

CHAPTER I.

THE BEEMAN

The road was a sunny, dusty one, leading upward through Medford Valley, with half-wooded hills on each side whose far outline quivered in the hot, breathless air of mid-June afternoon. Oliver Peyton seemed to have no regard for heat or dust, however, but trudged along with such a determined stride that people passing turned to look after him, and more than one swift motor car curved aside to give him room.

"Want a ride?" inquired one genial farmer, drawing up beside him. "Where are you going?"

Oliver turned to answer the first question, meaning to reply with a relieved "yes," but his square, sunburned face hardened at the second.

"Oh, I am just going down the road—a little way," he replied stiffly, shook his head at the repeated offer of a lift, and tramped on in the dust.

The next man he met seemed also to feel a curiosity as to his errand, for he stopped a very old, shambling horse to lean from his seat and ask point-blank: "Where may you be going in such a hurry on such a hot day?"

Oliver, looking up at the person who addressed him and gauging his close-set, hard gray eyes and his narrow, dark face, conceived an instant dislike and distrust of the stranger. He replied shortly, as he had before, but with less good temper:

"I am going down the road a little way. And, as you say, I am rather in a hurry."

"Oh, are you indeed?" returned the man, measuring the boy up and down with a disagreeable, inquisitive glance. "In too much of a hurry to have your manners with you, even!" He shot him a look of keen and hostile penetration. "It almost looks as though you were running away from something."

He stopped for no further comment but went jingling off in his rattletrap cart, the cloud of dust raised by his old horse's clumsy feet hanging long in the air behind him. Oliver plodded forward, muttering dark threats against the disagreeable stranger, and wishing that he had been sufficiently quick of speech to contradict him.

Yet the random guess was a correct one, and running away was just what Oliver was doing. He had not really meant to when he came out through the pillared gateway of his cousin's place; he had only thought that he would walk down the road toward the station—and see the train come in. Yet the resolve had grown within him as he thought of all that had passed in the last few days, and as he looked forward to what was still to come. As he walked down the road, rattling the money in his pockets, turning over his wrongs in his mind, the thought had come swiftly to him that he need no longer endure things as they were. It was three miles to the railroad station; but, once there, he could be whisked away from all the troubles that had begun to seem unendurable. The inviting whistle of a train seemed to settle the matter finally.

"It isn't as though I were afraid of anything," he reflected, looking back uneasily. "If I thought I were afraid I would never go away and leave Janet behind like this. No, I am only going because I will not be made to do what I hate."

He told himself this several times by way of reassurance, but seemed always to find it necessary to say it again. There were some strange things about the place where he and his younger sister Janet had come to make a visit, things that made him feel, even on the first day, that the whole house was haunted by some vague disquiet of which no one would tell him the cause. His Cousin Jasper had changed greatly since they had last seen him. He had always been a man of quick, brilliant mind but of mild and silent manners, yet now he was nervous, irritable, and impatient, in no sense a genial host.

Janet, Oliver's sister, had already begun to love the place, nor did she seem to notice the uneasiness that appeared to fill the house. She did not remember her cousin as well as did her brother and was thus less conscious of a change. So far, she had been spending her time very happily, being shown by Mrs. Brown, the housekeeper, through the whole of Cousin Jasper's great mansion and inspecting all the treasures that it contained. It was a new house, built only a year ago.

"And a real calamity it was when the work came to an end so soon," Mrs. Brown had said, "for it kept Mr. Peyton interested and happy all the time it was going on. We had hoped the south wing would be building these three months more."

Janet thought the great rooms were very beautiful, but Oliver did not like their vast silence in which the slightest sound seemed so disconcertingly loud. He was not used to such a quiet house, for their own home was a cozy, shabby dwelling, full of the stir and bustle and laughter of happy living. Here the boy found that noises would burst from him in the most unexpected and involuntary manner, noises that the long rooms and passageways seemed to take up and echo and magnify a hundred times. Mrs. Brown was constantly urging him "not to disturb poor Mr. Peyton," and Hotchkiss, the butler, who went about with silent footsteps, always looked pained when Oliver slammed a door or made a clatter on the stairs. He had never seen a butler before, except in the movies, so that he found the presence of Hotchkiss somewhat oppressive.

It was the change in his host, however, that had really spoiled the visit. Jasper Peyton was a cousin of his mother's, younger than she and very fond of her and her children. At their house he was always a much-desired guest, for he had "the fairy-godfather gift," as their mother put it, and was constantly doing delightful things for them. He was tall and spare, with a thin, sensitive face that, so it seemed to Oliver, was always smiling then, but that never smiled now.

The boy had noted a difference on the evening of their arrival, even as they drove up to the house through the warm darkness and the drifting fragrance of the June night.

"I can hardly remember how Cousin Jasper looks, but I think I will like his garden," Janet had observed, sniffing vigorously.

Oliver nodded, but he was not listening. He was looking up at the lighted house where the door stood open, with Hotchkiss waiting, and where he could see, through the long windows facing the terrace, that Cousin Jasper was hurrying through the library to meet them in the hall. Even at that distance their cousin did not look the same; he walked slower, he had lost his erect carriage and his old energy of action. He seemed a thin, high-shouldered ghost of his former self, with all spirit and cheerfulness gone out of him.

Janet and Oliver were paying their first visit without their mother, and, to guests of thirteen and fifteen respectively, such an occasion was no small cause for excitement. For that reason they were very slow to admit that they were not enjoying themselves, but the truth at last could not be denied. Cousin Jasper, preoccupied and anxious, left them almost completely to their own devices, neglected to provide any amusement for them, and seemed, at times, to forget even that they were there.

"You are a great comfort to him, my dears. He seems worried and distracted-like lately," Mrs. Brown had told them. "He does not like to be in this great house alone."

To Oliver it seemed that their presence meant very little, a fact which caused him to puzzle, to chafe and, finally, as was fairly natural, to grow irritated. After he and Janet had explored the house and garden, there seemed nothing left to do for Oliver but to stroll up and down the drive, stare through the tall gates at the motors going by, or to spend hours in the garage, sitting on a box and watching Jennings, the chauffeur, tinker with the big car that was so seldom used. Janet was able to amuse herself better, but her brother, by the third day, had reached a state of disappointed boredom that was almost ready, at any small thing, to flare out into open revolt. The very small thing required was the case of Cousin Eleanor.

They were all walking up and down the terrace on the third evening, directly after dinner, the boy and girl trying to accommodate their quick steps to Cousin Jasper's slower and less vigorous ones. Their host was talking little; Janet, with an effort, was attending politely to what he said, but Oliver was allowing his wits to go frankly woolgathering. It was still light enough to look across the slopes of the green valley and to see the shining silver river and the roofs of one or two big houses like their own, set each in its group of clustering trees. Beyond the stream, with its borders of yellow-green willows, there rose a smooth, round hill, bare of woods, or houses, with only one huge tree at the very top and with what seemed like a tiny cottage clinging to the slope just below the summit.

"Where that river bends at the foot of the hill, there ought to be rapids and good fishing," the boy was thinking. "Perhaps I might get over there to see, some day."

He was suddenly conscious, with a flush of guilt, that Cousin Jasper was asking him a question, but had stopped in the middle of a sentence, realizing that Oliver was not listening.

"So," he interrupted himself, "an old man's talk does not interest you, eh?"

He followed Oliver's glance down to the crooked river, and made an attempt to guess his thought.

"You were looking at that big stone house beyond the stream," he said, "and I suppose you were wondering who lives there."

He seemed to be making an effort to turn the conversation into more interesting channels, so that Oliver immediately gave him his full, but tardy attention.

"A cousin of mine owns the house. We are really all cousins or are related more or less, we who own the land in Medford Valley. But Tom Brighton is of closer kin to me than the others and I am very fond of him. We have both been too busy, just lately, to exchange as many visits as we used to do, but he has a daughter, Eleanor, just about your age, Oliver, a thoroughly nice girl, who would make a good playmate for both of you. I am neglecting your pleasure, I must have you meet her. You should see each other every day."

The suggestion seemed to afford Janet great delight; but, for some reason, it had the opposite effect upon Oliver. Perhaps Cousin Jasper did not know a great deal about younger people, perhaps he had not been taking sufficient note of the ways and feelings of this particular two, for it was quite certain that he had made a mistake. Oliver cared very little for girls, and to have this one thrust upon him unawares as a daily companion was not to his liking.

"It will be very nice for Janet," he remarked ungraciously, "but I—I don't have much to do with girls."

Some pure perversity made him picture his Cousin Eleanor as a prim young person, with sharp elbows and a pinched nose and stringy hair. She would be lifeless and oppressively good-mannered, he felt certain. All the ill success of the last three days seemed to be behind his sudden determination to have none of her. But Cousin Jasper, having once conceived the idea, was not to be gainsaid.

"No, I haven't been doing the proper thing for you. We will have Eleanor over to lunch to-morrow and you two shall go with Jennings in the car to fetch her. Don't protest, it won't be any trouble."

Later, as they went upstairs, Janet pleaded and argued with a thunderously rebellious Oliver who vowed and insisted that he would have no unknown female cousin thrust upon him.

"It is all right for you, Janet," he insisted, "but I won't have Cousin Jasper arranging any such thing for me. When I told him I didn't like girls, he should have listened. No, I don't care if it is wrong, I am going to tell him, to-morrow, just what I think."

Janet shook her brown, curly head in despair.

"I believe you will have to do what he says, in the end," she declared.

The next morning, at breakfast time, Oliver had not relented, for a night haunted by visions of this unknown cousin had in no way added to his peace of mind.

"I have been thinking about that girl you spoke about," he began, looking across the table and over the wide bowl of sweet peas to fix his cousin with a glance of firm determination, "and I don't really care to meet her. Janet can go to fetch her, but—you mustn't expect—I don't know how——"

His defense broke down and Cousin Jasper was ill-advised enough to laugh.

"Stuff and nonsense," he said. "If you are afraid of girls it is time you got over it. I have telephoned Eleanor already, but she couldn't come." Oliver brightened, but relapsed, the next moment, into deeper gloom than ever. "She said that she would be at home later in the afternoon, so you and Janet are to go over and call on her. I have ordered the motor for three o'clock."

It was Janet's suppressed giggle that added the last spark to Oliver's kindling anger. He was fond of his Cousin Jasper, he was troubled concerning him, and disturbed by the haunting feeling that something was wrong in the big house. Yet baffled anxiety often leads to irritation, and irritation, in Oliver's case, was being tactlessly pushed into rage. He said little, for he was a boy of few words, nor, so he told himself, could he really be rude to Cousin Jasper no matter how foolishly obstinate he was.

"But I'll get out of it somehow," he reflected stormily as he gulped down his breakfast and strode out into the garden. "I'll think of a way."

Cudgel his brains as he might, however, he could think of no plausible escape from the difficulty. He had found no excuse by lunch time, and was relieved that Cousin Jasper did not appear, being deep in some task in his study. At half past two Janet went upstairs to dress and Hotchkiss came to Oliver in the library to say:

"The car was to be ready at three o'clock, sir. Is that correct?"

To which Oliver replied desperately:

"Tell Jennings to make it half past three. I am going for a walk."

So he had plunged out through the gates and, once away down the dusty road, he became more and more of a rebel and finally a fugitive.

"I won't go back," he kept saying to himself. "I won't go back."

There was enough money in his pocket to take him home, and there was a train from the junction at three. He could telephone from there, very briefly, that he was going and that Hotchkiss was to send his things. He was beginning to discover some use for a butler, after all.

He trudged on, growing very hot, but feeling more and more relieved at the thought of escape. The way, however, was longer than he had imagined, and three o'clock came, with the station not yet in sight. There was another train at five, he remembered, but thought that it would be better not to spend the intervening time waiting openly on the platform. He would be missed long before then and Jennings and Janet, or perhaps even Cousin Jasper himself, would come to look for him. It would be better for him to cross the nearest meadow and spend the two hours in the woods, or he might settle the question over which he had been wondering, whether there were really fish in that sharp bend of the river.

He climbed a stone wall and dropped knee-deep into a field of hay and daisies. Toward the right, a quarter of a mile away, he could see the house of gray stone standing in the midst of wide, green gardens and approached by an elm-bordered drive. At that very moment he should have been rolling up to the door in Cousin Jasper's big car, to inquire for the much-detested Eleanor Brighton. He made a wry face at the thought and went hurrying down the slope of the hayfield, passed through a grove of oak and maple trees, and reached the river. It was a busy, swift little stream, talking to itself among the tall grasses as the current swept down toward the sea. A rough bridge spanned it just below the bend, and here he could stand and see the fish; for they were there, as he had thought. In the absence of fishing tackle, he could only watch them, but the sound of a car, passing on a road near by, made him hurry on.

Now, he felt, he was away from passers-by indeed! Another stone wall, patterned with lichen, separated him from the briar-filled wilderness of an old, abandoned orchard. Each one of the twisted apple trees looked at least a thousand years of age, so bent, gnarled, and misshapen had it become. Through the straight rows he could look up the slope of the round hill that he had so often watched from Cousin Jasper's garden, he could make out the roof line of the tiny, dilapidated cottage, and could see that the big tree at the summit was an oak. The orchard was a deserted waste and the house seemed uninhabited. Yet just below the summit, the hill was dotted with small, boxlike structures, painted white, that might have been chicken houses, but seemed scarcely large enough. Filled with curiosity, he went forward to investigate, munching, as he went, a yellow June apple that he had picked up in the grass.

A rough lane opened before him, that passed through the orchard and wound up the hill, with its high grass trodden a little as though, after all, people did sometimes pass that way. He had climbed only a little way when he heard voices.

The tumble-down cottage was not empty, as he had thought, for two people were standing in the doorway. He stopped abruptly. The man in worn overalls and the girl beside him, with her bobbed hair, bright eyes, and faded pink gingham apron, did not look like a very forbidding pair. But Oliver's uneasy conscience made him feel that any person he met might guess his plans in some mysterious way and interfere with his escape. Very quietly he turned about and began to hurry down the hill. He had retreated too late, however, for the man had seen him and proceeded to call after him in what seemed a very peremptory tone:

"Stop!"

For a moment, Oliver hesitated, uncertain whether to obey or to take to his heels and seek safety in the wood below. Could the man have read his secret, or was the apple in his hand the cause of the summons? Before he could really decide, the girl's voice was raised also—pleading and urgent.

"We need you," she called. "You must help us. Oh, don't go away!"

He turned slowly and went toward them through the tall grass, uncertain, suspicious, afraid even yet that he might fall into some trap that would delay his flight. His uneasiness was not in any way quieted by his seeing that one of the white boxes stood, uncovered, before the two and that it was a beehive.

"You have come just in time," said the man, "if you are willing to help us. It is a difficult business, hiving a swarm of bees at this season, and Polly, here, is no use at all. This is her first day with the bees this

The Windy Hill

year, and she jumps up and down when they sing around her head, and that stops everything."

"I do better usually," the girl confessed humbly, "but I forget, over the winter, how to be quiet and calm when a million bees are buzzing in my ear."

She thrust into Oliver's hand the leather and metal bellows that blows wood smoke into the hive, and her father began giving him directions as unconcernedly as though his helping were a matter of course.

"Just stand beside me, stay very still, and keep blowing smoke; that is right. Don't move and never mind how close the bees come. There is no danger of your being stung."

The square white box was full of wooden frames, hanging one behind another, like the leaves of a book. One by one the man lifted them out, swept off the black curtain of bees that clung to them, and showed the clean, new, sweet-smelling honeycomb.

"When an old hive gets too crowded, and the bees begin to swarm," he explained, "we divide them and put some frames and bees into a new, empty hive. See them going to work already, and look at that piece of comb that has just been built; one would think that the fairies had made it."

Oliver had never seen anything so white and thin and delicate as the frail new cells ready for the fresh honey. He forgot any dread of the myriad creatures buzzing about his head, he forgot even his plan, and his impatience of delay. He bent to peer into the hive, to examine the young bees just hatching, the fat, black, and brown drones and the slim, alert queen bee. The girl, now that the responsibility of helping was off her hands, forgot her own nervousness and pressed forward also to look and ask questions. She must be about thirteen or fourteen years old, was Oliver's vague impression of her; she had dark hair and quick, brown eyes, her cheeks were very pink, and one of them was decorated with a black smudge from the smoke blower. He was too intent to notice her much or to remember his fearful dread of girls. And of course this little thing in the shabby apron was very different from the threatened Cousin Eleanor.

He could not see much of the man's face under the worn straw hat, as they bent over the hive, but he liked the slow, drawling voice that answered his innumerable questions and he found the chuckling laugh irresistibly infectious. The stranger's brown hands moved with steady skill among the horde of crawling insects, until the last frame was set in place, the last puff of smoke blown, and the cover was put down.

"There, young man," said the beekeeper, "that was a good job well done, thanks to you; but you must not go yet. Polly and I always have a little lunch here in the honey house when we have finished, to revive us after our exhausting labor."

Oliver was about to protest that he must go on at once, but the man interrupted him, with a twinkle in his eye.

"There is a spring behind the house where we wash up," he said. "Polly will give you some soap and a towel. Wood smoke smells good, but it is just as black as the soft-coal kind."

When he looked at himself a moment later in the mirror of the spring, Oliver realized that he was scarcely fit to start on a journey, since, in his energetic wielding of the smoker he had smudged his face far worse than even Polly had. He began splashing and scrubbing, but honey and soot and the odd, sticky glue with which bees smear their hives are none of them easy to remove. When he presented himself once more at the door of the cottage, there was a feast spread out on the rough table—buttered and toasted biscuits spread with honey, iced cocoa with whipped cream, and a big square chocolate cake. Quite suddenly he remembered how far he had walked and how hungry he was and with equal suddenness forgot his pressing necessity for setting off again. He sat down on the three-legged stool that the Beeman offered him, sampled the hot biscuit and the cold drink, and breathed a deep, involuntary sigh of content. In the presence of these friendly, shabbily dressed strangers he felt, for the first time since leaving home, really happy and at ease.

It seemed dark and cool within the little cottage after the blazing sunshine outside. The place was evidently no longer used for anything but a storehouse and a shelter for picnics of this kind, but it was a quaint, attractive little dwelling and evidently very old. The main room where they sat had a big-beamed ceiling, deep casement windows, and a door that swung open in two sections, one above the other. The upper half was wide open now, framing a sun-bathed picture of the green slope, the treetops of the orchard, and the rising hills opposite, with a narrow glimpse of sparkling, blue sea. The air was very hot and quiet, with the sleepy peacefulness that belongs to summer afternoons. The round, dense shadow of the oak tree above them was lengthening so that its cool tip just touched the doorstone.

Polly, with hands as brown and skillful as her father's, was still toasting biscuits before the little fire they had built on the rough hearth. The Beeman, having taken off his hat, showed a handsome, cheery face much like his daughter's, except that his big nose was straight, rather than tilted like her small one, and his eyes were gray. Their clothes were even older and shabbier than Oliver had at first observed, but their manners were so easy and cordial that the whole of the little house seemed filled with the pleasant atmosphere of friendliness.

Polly left the fire at last, bringing a plate of hot biscuits, and sat down beside the table.

"Daddy always tells me a story when we have finished with the bees," she began a little shyly. "He said he had one saved up in his head that I would especially like. You won't mind our going on with it, will you?"

Oliver would not mind at all. He felt assured already that he would like anything that the Beeman had to say.

"I suppose you must have it, if your heart is set on it," Polly's father said, "but my tales are usually designed for an audience of only one. This young gentleman may not like our style of stories, my dear."

"I hope he will," replied Polly, "but—oh, daddy, I forgot all about it, didn't we have an engagement some time about now, at home?"

"No," he returned so positively that his daughter, though at first a little puzzled, seemed quite satisfied. "It is quite all right for us to stay here."

He chuckled for a moment, as though over some private joke of his own, then at last laid down his pipe and crossed his legs. Oliver leaned back against the wall and Polly curled up on the bench by the fireplace.

"Are you both quite comfortable?" the Beeman inquired. "Very well, then I'll begin."

CHAPTER II.

THE SEVEN BROTHERS OF THE SUN

Nashola did not live in fairyland, although there were seasons when his country was so beautiful that it might well have belonged to some such enchanted place. He did not know whether he loved it best when the thickets were all in bloom with pink crab apple and the brown, wintry hills had put on their first spring green, or when every valley was scarlet and golden with frost-touched maple trees in the autumn. But to-day it was neither, being hot midsummer, with the wild grass thick and soft on the slope of the hill that he was climbing, and with the heavy foliage of the oak tree on the summit rustling in a hot, fitful breeze. It was high noontide with the sunlight all about him, yet Nashola walked warily and looked back more than once at his comrades who had dared follow him only halfway up the hill. His was no ordinary errand, for, all about him, Nashola felt dangers that he could neither hear nor see. Before him, sitting motionless as a statue, with his back against the trunk of the oak tree and his keen, hawk-like face turned toward the hills and the sky, was Secotan, the sorcerer and medicine man, whom all of Nashola's tribe praised, revered, and dreaded.

None but the full-grown warriors used to venture to have speech with him, and then only as he sat in the door of his lodge, with the men in a half circle before him. They never came alone. Along all the seaboard, the Indians talked of Secotan, the man most potent in spells and charms and prophecies, who was said to talk with strange spirits in his lodge by night and who could call up storms out of the sea at will. This spot at the summit of the hill, where the medicine man sat so often, sometimes muttering spells, sometimes staring straight before him across the valley, was magic forbidden ground, where no one but himself was known to come. Yet the young Nashola, only fifteen years old, and far from being a warrior, had been told that he must consult the medicine man and had been in too much haste to seek him in his own lodge or to wait until he could persuade a comrade to go with him.

Stretched along the river below them was the camp of Nashola's brown-skinned people, where springs gave them fresh water and where the eastern hills of the valley gave shelter from the winter storms that blew in from the sea. Beyond those green hills were rocky slopes, salt swamps, a stretch of yellow sand, and then the great Atlantic rollers, tumbling in upon the beach. The Indians of Nashola's village would go thither sometimes to dig for clams, to fish from the high rocks, and even, on occasions, to swim in the breakers close to shore. But they were land-abiding folk, they feared nothing in the forest, and would launch their canoes in the most headlong rapids of the inland rivers; yet there was dread and awe in their eyes when they looked out upon the sea. Not one of them had ever ventured beyond the island at the mouth of the harbor.

They were a shifting, wandering people, moving here and there with the seasons, as the deer and moose moved their grazing grounds, but their most settled abiding place was this little green valley where they spent a part of every year. Sometimes word would come drifting in, through other tribes, of strange, white-faced men who had landed on their shores, but who always sailed away again, since this was still the time when America was all the Indians' own. What they did not see troubled them little and they went on, undisturbed, hunting and fishing and paying their vows to

The Windy Hill

the spirits and demons that they thought to be masters of their little world.

The old, wrinkled squaw who was Nashola's grandmother was the only one of them all who seemed oppressed with care. The boy, whose parents were dead, was her special charge and was not, as he should be, like other Indian lads. He was slim and swift and was as skillful as his companions with the bow and spear, but he had a strange love for running along the sea beach with the waves snatching at his bare, brown legs, and he was really happy only when he was swimming in the green water. The day he swam to the island and back again, paying no heed to the shouts and warnings of his friends, and declaring, when he landed, that he would have gone farther save that the tide had turned—that day had brought his old grandmother's patience to an end.

"It is not fitting that one of our tribe should be so familiar with the sea," she stormed at him. "We were not born to master that wild salt water; the gods that rule us have said over and over again that the woods and rivers are ours, but that we are to have no dealings with the spirits of the sea. Since I cannot make you listen, you shall talk to some one who will. You shall go to ask the medicine man if what I say is not so."

Nashola had come, therefore, to ask his question, but he found that it needed a bold heart to advance, without quaking, into that silent presence and to speak out with Secotan's black eyes seeming to stare him through and through.

"Is it true," he began, "that men of our tribe should have no trust in the sea? My grandmother says that I should hate it and fear it, but I do not. Must I learn to be afraid?"

Slowly the man nodded.

Most Indians grow old quickly, and are withered like dried-up apples as soon as the later years come upon them. But Secotan, although his hair was gray, had still the clear-cut face with its arched nose and heavy brows of a younger man. Only his eyes, deep, piercing, and very wise, seemed to show how long he had lived and how much he had learned.

"Our fathers and their fathers before them have always known that we must distrust the sea," he said at last. "No matter how blue and smiling it may be it can never be our friend. We may swim near the shore, we may even launch our canoes and journey, if the way be short, from one harbor to another when the sky is clear and the winds are asleep. But always we are to remember that the sea is our enemy and a treacherous enemy in the end."

He turned away to stare at the hills again, but Nashola lingered, not yet satisfied. It was unheard-of boldness to question Secotan's words, yet the boy could not keep his hot protests to himself.

"But is it not wrong to pretend to fear what we do not?" he objected. "Do the spirits of the water actually rise up and tell you that we must keep to the shore? I do not believe it, although my grandmother says so until my ears ring again."

Secotan turned his head quickly, as though to hide the ghost of a smile.

"The voices of the wind and the breakers and of the thunder all cry the same message," he declared, "and wise men have learned that it warns them to hug the land. You must heed your grandmother, even though her words are shrill and often repeated."

He would say no more, so Nashola went away, pondering his answer as he walked down the hill. After all, no harm had come to him from entering the medicine man's presence unbidden, as his comrades had all said. He answered their questions very shortly as they came crowding about him, and to the persistent queries of his grandmother he would say nothing at all. Yet the others noticed that his canoe lay unused in the shelter of a rock on the sandy beach where he had left it, and that he swam in the sea no more.

The days passed, the hot, quiet summer passing with them. One evening, as they all sat about the camp fire, one of the older warriors said quietly:

"The time is near when our medicine man must go from us."

"Why?" questioned Nashola's grandmother, while the boy turned quickly to hear.

"He has not sat upon the hill nor before the door of his lodge for three days, and the venison and corn we have carried to him have lain untouched for all that time. One of us who ventured close heard a cry from within and groaning. It may be that he must die."

"But will no one help him?" cried Nashola. It was not proper that a boy should speak out in the presence of the older warriors, but he could not keep his wonder to himself.

"There is danger to common folk in passing too close to the medicine man's lodge," his grandmother explained quickly. "There are spirits within who are his friends but who might destroy us. And when he is ill unto death and the beings from another world have come to bear his soul away, then must no man go near."

"Sometimes a medicine man has a companion to whom he teaches his wisdom and who takes his place when he is gone," said the man by the fire. "But even that comrade flees away when death is at hand and the spirits begin to stand close about his master. Yes, such a man must die alone."

All through the night Nashola lay awake, thinking of what he had heard. Secotan was, he knew, a man of powerful magic, but he could not forget that there was a look in his eyes and a kindliness in his tone that seemed human, after all. Must he suffer and die there, without help, merely because he was greater and wiser than the rest? Or, when death came close and the host of unearthly beings gathered about him, would he not feel it of comfort to have a living friend by his side? It was long past midnight and in the black darkness that comes before day, before the boy came to final resolution.

He crawled out from under the shelter of his lodge and slipped noiselessly through the sleeping camp. Every rustle in the grass, every stirring leaf in the thicket made him jump and shiver, yet he kept steadily on. The sharp outline of Secotan's pointed lodge poles stood out against the stars, halfway up the shoulder of the hill. The door showed black and open as he came near, but there was no sound from within. The only thing that seemed alive was a dull, glowing coal in the ashes of a fire that was not quite dead. The boy stooped down before the door and spoke in a shaking voice:

"Secotan, Secotan, do you still live?"

A hollow, gasping whisper sounded from the shadows within:

"I am living, but death is very near."

Nashola stood still for a moment. He could picture that gaunt figure lying helpless on the ground, with the darkness all about peopled by strange shapes visible to the sorcerer's eyes alone, crowding spirits come to carry him away to an unknown world. But even as a wave of icy terror swept over him, he remembered how fearful it would be to lie all alone in that haunted darkness, and he bent low and slipped through the door.

"I know that all the spirits of the earth and air and water are with you," he said as he felt his way to the deerskin bed and sat down beside it, "but I thought, among them all, you might wish for a friend beside you who was flesh and blood."

A quivering hand was laid for an instant on his knee.

"There is no man who does not feel terror when he comes to die alone," the medicine man whispered, "and Secotan is less of a man than you."

Through the dragging hours Nashola sat beside him, listening with strained ears to every sound—the soft moving of a snake through the grass before the door, the nibbling of a field mouse at the skin of the tent, the sharp scream of a bird in the wood captured by a marauding owl. The blackness grew thinner at last, showing the lodge poles, the shabby skins of the bed, and finally the sick man's face, drawn and haggard with pain. As the dawn came up over the hills, he opened his eyes and spoke:

"Bring those herbs that hang against the lodge pole and build up the fire. When the stones about it are hot, wrap them in wet blankets and lay them in the tent. The gods may have decreed that I am to live."

Nashola worked frantically all through the day. He filled the lodge with steam from the hot stones, he brewed bitter drafts of herbs and held them to Secotan's lips once in every hour by the sun. After a long time he saw the fever ebb, saw the man's eyes lose their strange glittering, and heard his voice gather strength each time he spoke. For three nights and days the boy nursed him, all alone in the lodge, with men bringing food to leave at the door but with no one willing to come inside. When at last Nashola went back to his own dwelling, Secotan was sitting, by his fire, weak and thin, but fairly on the way to health again.

The friendship that had grown up during that night of suffering and terror seemed to become deeper and deeper as time passed. There was scarcely a day when Nashola did not climb the hill in the late afternoon to sit under the rustling oak tree and talk for a long hour with the medicine man. His companions of his own age looked askance at such a friendship and his grandmother begged and scolded, but without avail.

Almost always, as he sat with his back against the tree, or lay full length in the long grass that was beginning to be dry and yellow with the coming autumn, the boy would fix his eyes upon the hills opposite through which there showed a gleam of sea. Like the picture of some forbidden thing was that glint of blue, framed by the green slopes and the sky above. He could see the whitecaps, the dancing glimmer of the sun, and the gray sea gulls that whirled and hovered and dipped before his longing gaze. He would lift his head to sniff the salt breeze that swept through the cleft in the hills, and to listen for that far-off thunder that could sometimes be heard as the great waves broke on the beach. At last, one day when he had sat so long with his friend that dusk was falling and the stars were coming out, he broke through the silence with a sudden question:

"Secotan, what lies beyond that sea?"

The medicine man shook his head without speaking.

"My grandmother says 'Nothing,'" pursued Nashola, "but I know that cannot be. Is it one of the things that I must not ask and that you may not tell me because you are a sorcerer and I am only a boy?"

Secotan was silent so long that Nashola thought he did not mean to reply at all. Even when he spoke it did not seem to be an answer.

"Do you see those seven stars?" he said, "that are rising from the sea and that march so close together that you keep thinking they are going to melt into one?"

"Yes," answered the boy. "I often lie before our lodge door and watch them go up the sky. There are bigger stars all about them, but somehow I love those the best, they are so small and bright and seem to look down on us with such friendly eyes."

"It is told among the medicine men," Secotan went on slowly, "that many, many moons ago, long before this oak tree grew upon this hill, before its father's father had yet been planted as an acorn, our people came hither across just such a sea as that. Far to the westward it lay, and they came, a mere handful of bold spirits in their canoes, across a wide water from some land that we have utterly forgotten. Some settled down at once upon the shores of the waters they had crossed, but some pressed eastward, little by little, as the generations passed. They filled the land with their children and in the end they came to another sea and went no farther. But the men who had led them were of a different heart than ours; there were always some who were not content to hunt and fish and move only as the deer move or as the seasons change. They wished to press on, ever on, to let nothing stop the progress of their march. It is said that when they came to this sea there were seven brothers who, when their people would no longer follow, launched their canoes and set off once more to the eastward, and never came back.

"They dwell there in the sky, we think, and they shine through those months of autumn that are dearest of all the year to our people, when the days are warm and golden before the winter, when the woods are bare and hunting is easy, when the game is fat from the summer grazing and our yellow corn is ripe. They come back to us in the Hunter's Moon and they watch over us all through the cold winter. We call them the Seven Brothers of the Sun."

Nashola was silent, waiting, for he knew from his friend's voice that there was more that he wished to say.

"Your mother, who is dead, was not of our blood, they tell me. Your father took her from another tribe and they had brought her captive, from the north of us, so that she is no kin of ours. Sometimes I think that there must have run in her veins the blood of those seven brothers and that, in you, their bold spirit lives again. There is no one of your kind who loves the sea as you do, who has no shadow of a fear of it. And you are first, in all my life, who has asked me what lay beyond."

"I should like," said Nashola steadily, still watching the gray water and the gleam of stars above it, "I should like to go and see."

"Often I have wondered," the man went on, his voice growing very earnest, "whether you would not like to come to dwell with me, to learn the lore that makes me a medicine man and to take my place when I must go. I, who was taught by the wisest of us all, have waited long to find some one worthy of that teaching, and able to hold the power that I have. You can be a greater man than I, Nashola; not only your whole tribe will do your bidding and hang upon your words, but the men of our race all up and down the coast will revere you and talk of you as the greatest sorcerer ever known. Will you come to my lodge, will you learn from me, will you follow in my way?"

Nashola tried to speak, choked and tried again.

"I cannot do it," he said huskily.

"Why?"

There was a sharp note of wonder, hurt friendship, even of terror, in the man's voice.

"The people of our village say you are not like other men," said the boy. "They say you can call the friendly spirits of the forest and the hostile gods of the sea, and that you have wisdom learned in another world. But I, who am your friend, think it is not so. I love you dearly, but I know you are a man as I am. I know the sea is only water and that the forest is only trees. I—I do not believe."

He got to his feet, blind with misery, and went stumbling down the hill. The warm September darkness was thick about him, but up on the hill the starlight showed plainly the motionless figure sitting beneath the oak tree, never turning to look after him, uttering no sound of protest or reproach.

As September days passed into October, as the Seven Brothers rode higher in the sky, strange tales, once again, began to come from the south. More white men had been seen in their ships, sailing up and down the coast, trading with the Indians, buying the fish that they had caught and trying to talk to them in an unknown tongue.

"We have heard stories before and will hear them again," said the older warriors incredulously. "Such tales are of the sort that old women tell about the fires on winter nights."

"What does your friend the medicine man say of these rumors, Nashola?" asked one of the boys of his own age, but Nashola did not answer. He went no more up the hill to the big oak tree; he had held no speech for weeks with Secotan. Yet he would suffer no one to ask him why.

A day came when the news could no longer be disbelieved. A boy of the tribe, who had been digging for clams on the beach, came running home with startling tidings.

"The white men—the winged canoes—as big as our lodges——" he gasped. "Come quickly and see!"

Old men and young, squaws and papooses, every one deserted the little settlement by the river and went in wild haste up the eastward hills to look upon this strange wonder. It was a lowering day with overcast skies and water of a sullen gray and with ominously little wind. In speechless wonder the Indians stood gazing, for there indeed were three white-sailed ships, moving slowly before the lazy breeze, stanch little fishing vessels of English build, come to see whether this unexplored stretch of coast would yield them any cargo. As they watched, the largest one got up more sail, veered away upon a new tack, and was followed by the others.

"What can they be? Are they come to destroy us all?" asked a trembling old woman, and no one could answer.

"Hush," said another in a moment, "the medicine man is coming."

Secotan, who so seldom left his own lodge now, and who never mixed with the village folk, was climbing slowly up the hill after them. Nashola noticed that he had begun to look old, that his fierce hawk's face was sunken, and that he walked very slowly, leaning upon his staff. The men and women drew back respectfully as he advanced and stood in a silent, waiting circle, while he shaded his eyes and gazed long at the ships, now growing smaller in the distance.

"Are they friends or enemies, Secotan?" one of the hunters ventured to ask, but the medicine man replied only:

"That must be as the gods decree."

"Then destroy them for us," cried the old squaw, Nashola's grandmother. "Call up a storm that will break their wings and shatter the sides of those giant canoes. Bring wind and rain and thunder and all the spirits of the sea to overwhelm them."

There was a breathless silence as Secotan slowly moved forward and raised his staff. Nashola, standing before the other boys, watched the medicine man's face with eyes that never wavered. Even as the sorcerer moved there came a low mutter of thunder across the gray, level floor of the sea, and a distant streak of darker water showed the coming wind.

"There is the storm! The very winds obey him!"

The cry went up from all the Indians, save only Nashola who stood silent. The medicine man turned to look at him, then hesitated and dropped his eyes.

"Why do you wait? Raise up a hurricane, O greatest of sorcerers," cried a man behind them.

"No," shouted Secotan suddenly. He flung down his staff and held up his empty hands before his face. "I will raise no storm," he cried, "I will call no spirits from the deep—because I cannot. The wind and thunder answer no man's bidding—storms come and go at the will of the Great Spirit alone. There is one soul here that I love, one being whom, in all my life, I have had for a friend. In his eyes I will stand for truth at last, although I had almost learned to believe in my magic myself. I can do none of those things that you think. I am a man without power, like every one of you!"

A roar of anger went up, a dull, savage, guttural sound that died away almost at once into silence, a quiet more ominous than an outcry could have been. Terrified by that strange apparition out yonder upon the waters, the Indians saw themselves deserted by the one person to whom they could look for courage and counsel. Only half understanding, they knew, at least, that Nashola had been the means of their medicine man's downfall. Frenzied hands seized them both and dragged them headlong down toward the water. Visions of the savage tortures that his people wreaked upon their enemies passed through the boy's mind, but he did not struggle or cry out, although Secotan's set face, beside him, turned gray under its coppery skin. Some one had found Nashola's canoe, left long unused upon the beach, and had launched it in the breakers.

"Let him go back to the sea that he loved, this boy who has never been one of us. Let the man perish in the storm that is coming without his call."

Relentless hands flung them into the frail boat and pushed it out through the surf. Nashola crawled to the stern and took up the paddle; a crash of thunder broke over their heads and a wild flare of lightning lit the dark water as he dipped the blade. In a moment, rain was falling in blinding sheets, the wind and spray were roaring in their ears, and the ebbing tide was carrying them away, out of the harbor, past the rocky island, straight to the open, angry sea.

After a long time, Secotan, who had lain inert where he had been thrown into the boat, got to his knees and took up the second paddle. Only by keeping the little boat's bow to the wind could immediate destruction be averted. But the medicine man's strokes were feeble, affording little help, and at last he laid down the blade.

"It is of no use, Nashola," he said. "Death rides on the wind and snatches at us from the black waters. Lay down your paddle and let us die."

"No," the boy answered, "even though death is not an hour away, we will fight it until the very end."

Darkness shut down about them so that they could scarcely see each other as they went on in silence. Although each combing, foam-capped rush of water seemed certain to overwhelm them, there was a strange exhilaration, a mad thrill in rising to every giant wave and shooting down its green side in a cloud of spray. One—two—three—each one seemed the last, and yet there were ever more. Nashola's arms were numb and heavy, his head reeled, but still he struggled on. He wished at last that death would come quickly, to still the terrible aching weariness that possessed his whole being. The worst of the storm had blown, roaring, past them, but the seas were still heavy and nothing—nothing, Nashola thought, could ever bring back the strength to his failing arms.

Suddenly the clouds were torn apart, showing a glimmer of stars and a vague glimpse of the tossing black water all about them.

"Look, look, Nashola," cried the medicine man, pointing upward, "they have come to help us, your kinsmen, the Seven Brothers of the Sun!"

But Nashola was not looking at the sky; his eyes were fixed on a ghostly shape moving close ahead of them and on the fitful gleam of a ship's lantern that tossed and glimmered in the dark. Dropping his paddle he put his hands to his mouth and lifted his voice in a long hail. The light bobbed and swung and an answering shout came through the darkness.

To the weather-beaten English sailors, used to the rough adventures of sailing new and uncharted seas, there was little excitement in picking up two half-drowned Indians, although they had never done such a thing before. They warmed the two with blankets, they revived them with fiery remedies, and they sat about them on the deck, trying to talk to them by means of signs, but with small success.

"It is no common thing to see these natives so far from shore," the

The Windy Hill

mate said to the captain, "for as a rule the Indians distrust the sea. We cannot find out how these came to be adrift in that canoe. The young one tries to make us understand, but the old man merely covers his face and groans. I think he will not believe that we are men like himself."

"Bring the boy to me," the captain ordered. "Perhaps we may be able to understand him."

In the quiet dawn, when calm had followed the night's storm, the ship ran in toward a rocky headland to send a boat ashore. Yet when it had been lowered and Secotan had dropped into it, he turned to see Nashola standing on the deck above, making no move to follow.

"I am not coming, Secotan," he declared steadily. "The chief of these men and I have talked with signs and he wishes to carry me to his home on this strange winged vessel. He promises that he will bring me safe back again. Then I can tell you and all of our tribe what these white men really are. And I have always longed to know what lay beyond this forbidden sea."

Secotan did not protest.

"I have called you friend, I have wished to have you for my brother," he said, "but I must call you master now, since you have dared what I can never dare."

Much has been said of the courage of those white men who crossed the stormy Atlantic in their little vessels to explore an unknown continent. But what of the brave hearts of those Indians who thought the white men were spirits come out of the sea, who did not know what ships were, yet who still dared to set sail with them? For we know that there were such dusky voyagers, that they crossed the sea more than once in the English fishing vessels, and that they brought back to their own people almost unbelievable tales of cities and palaces, or harbors crowded with shipping and of whole countrysides covered with green, tilled fields. With all these wonders, however, they could tell their comrades that these white beings were mere men like themselves, to be neither hated nor dreaded as spirits of another world. Deep dwelling in Nashola was that born leadership that makes real men see through the long-established doubts and terrors of their race, who can distinguish the false from the true, who can go forward through shadowy perils to the clear light of knowledge and success.

It was in recognition of this that old Secotan, half understanding, wholly unable to put his feeling into words, standing alone upon the headland, raised his arms in reverent salute and cried a last good-by to his comrade:

"Farewell and good fortune, O Brother of the Sun!"

CHAPTER III.

JOHN MASSEY'S LANDLORD

The story had come to an end, but the boy and girl still waited as though to hear more.

"But do oak trees grow to be so old?" Oliver inquired at last, looking out at the moving shadow of the great tree that had now covered the doorstone.

"Yes, three hundred years is no impossible age for an oak. All the old grants of land speak of an oak tree on this hill as one of the landmarks."

"How did you know?" began Oliver, and then broke off, with a sudden jerk of recollection: "Oh, I forgot all about it—my train!"

He snatched out his watch and stood regarding it with a rueful face. He had missed the train by more than half an hour.

"Were you going away?" asked Polly sympathetically. "We are always missing trains like that, daddy and I. Won't they be surprised to see you come back!"

"They—they didn't know I was going," returned Oliver. "They are wondering now where I am." He was too much agitated to keep from doing his thinking out loud. "I must be getting back. Thank you for the story. Good-by."

He was gone before they could say more, leaving Polly, in fact, with her mouth open to speak and with the Beeman looking after him with an amused and quizzical grin, as though he recognized the symptoms of an uneasy conscience.

"We never asked him to come again," Polly lamented.

To which her father answered, "I believe he will come, just the same."

The smooth machinery of Cousin Jasper's house must have been thrown out of gear for a moment when the car came round to the door and Oliver failed to appear. It was running quietly and noiselessly again, however, by the time he returned. Janet was curled up in a big armchair in the library, enjoying a book, when he came in. She looked up at him rather curiously, but only said:

"Eleanor Brighton's mother telephoned at half past three that Eleanor had been detained somewhere, she didn't quite know where. She was very apologetic and hoped we would come some other time. I walked down the road to look for you, but you weren't in sight. I met such a strange man, coming in at the gate; he turned all the way around on the seat of his cart to stare at me. I didn't like him."

She did not press Oliver with questions and, as a result, he sat down beside her and told her the whole tale of his afternoon's adventures, with a glowing description of the Beeman and Polly.

"I must take you there to see them," he said, "I can't wait to show you how things look from that hill. And you should see the bees, and the little house, and hear the wind in the big tree. We will go to-morrow."

When Cousin Jasper appeared for dinner, Oliver felt somewhat apprehensive, but to his relief no questions were asked him. Their cousin listened rather absently while Janet explained why the proposed visit had not been made, and he offered no comment. He looked paler even than usual, with deeper lines in his face, and he sat at the end of the long table, saying little and eating less. Afterward he sat with them in the library, still restless and uneasy and speaking only now and then, in jerking sentences that they could scarcely follow. It was an evident relief to all three of them when the time came to say good night.

Oliver looked back anxiously over his shoulder, as their cousin returned to his study and as they, at the other end of the long room, went out into the hall.

"Something has happened to upset him more than usual," he said. "Do you think he could have guessed what I intended to do?"

Janet shook her head emphatically.

"He couldn't have guessed," she declared. "Even now I can hardly believe it of you, myself, Oliver."

Oliver, rather ashamed, was beginning to wonder at himself also.

They had fallen into the habit of going upstairs early to the comfortable sitting room into which their bedrooms opened. It was their own domain, a pleasant, breezy place, with deep wicker chairs, gay chintz curtains, flower boxes, and wide casements opening on a balcony. They had both found some rare treasures among the books downstairs and liked to carry them away for an hour of enjoyment before it was bedtime.

Oliver settled himself comfortably beside a window, opened his book, but did not immediately begin to read. His eyes wandered about the perfectly appointed room, stared out at the moonlit garden, and then came back to his sister.

"Why aren't we happy here, Janet?" he questioned. "It seems as though we had everything to make us so."

"Because he isn't happy," returned his sister, with a gesture toward the study where Cousin Jasper, distraught, worried, and forlorn, must even then be sitting alone.

"But why isn't he happy? There is everything here that he could wish for." Oliver added somewhat bitterly, after a pause: "Why don't grown-up people tell us things? It is miserable to be old enough to notice when affairs go wrong but not to be old enough to have them explained."

"Perhaps," said Janet hopefully, "we will be able to prove that we deserve to know. I think that you will, anyway, and then you can tell me."

It was not only the younger members of the household who were struggling with mystery that night, however. Before they had been reading many minutes, there came a discreet tap at the door and Hotchkiss appeared upon the threshold. Oliver was wondering what a boy unused to butlers was supposed to say or do on the occasion of such a visit, and even Janet, better at guessing the etiquette of such matters, seemed at a loss. And so also was Hotchkiss, as it presently began to be evident.

If the butler had been of the regulation variety, he might perhaps have known how to ask a few respectful questions without a change of his professional countenance and have gained his information without betraying its significance. But as it was, he had for the moment put off the wooden, expressionless face that he was supposed to wear at his work, and was openly anxious and disturbed.

"We're troubled about Mr. Peyton, Mrs. Brown and I," he began, coming frankly to the point at once. "He had a queer visitor to-day, one who has just been coming lately and who always leaves him upset. I wonder if you saw him, a thin man with a brown face and a kind of a way with him, somehow, in spite of his bad clothes."

"Did he drive a shambling old horse?" inquired Oliver, remembering suddenly the person he had noticed on the road, "and a wagon that rattled as though it were twenty years old? Yes, we both saw him."

"Had you ever seen him before?" Hotchkiss asked eagerly, and seemed disappointed when Oliver replied:

"No, we had never laid eyes on him before to-day."

"It is just in the last few weeks that he has been coming here so often," the man went on. "Before that he came rarely and we didn't think so much about him. I can remember the first time I saw him, soon after I had come

The Windy Hill

to Mr. Peyton, a year ago. The fellow rang the bell as bold as anything, but when I saw that rickety outfit drawn up to the steps, I was about to tell him that the other entrance was the place for him. He must have read my eye—he's a sharp one—for he said, 'Your master won't thank you for turning me away, when I'm a member of the family,' and sure enough, there was Mr. Peyton behind me in the hall telling me to bring him in. He was nervous and put out with everybody after the man was gone, and he is more and more upset each time he comes. And the fellow begins to come often. I thought that if he was a member of the family you might know who he was—and how we could get rid of him."

The heat of the last words put an end to any possible thought that the man's questions were prompted by a servant's unwarranted curiosity concerning his master. It was plain that Cousin Jasper was a well-beloved employer and that the two chief persons of his household had been laying their heads together over the mystery of his evident trouble.

Hotchkiss was about to tell them more, when a bell, sounding below, summoned him away. There was an interval during which they tried to return to their books, but found their minds occupied with thoughts of what the butler had said. Who could this man be, whom they had both noticed and both set down as odious, and whose coming seemed to have such an unhappy effect upon Cousin Jasper? A relative? It did not seem possible. Presently Hotchkiss was at the door again, more troubled than ever.

"Mr. Peyton wants the motor, but it's Jennings' evening off and he has gone to town," he said. "Didn't I hear you tell him, Mr. Oliver, that you knew how to drive that make of car?"

Oliver had, indeed, dropped such a hint two days before, hoping that the dullness of his visit might be lightened by his being invited to take the car out for a spin. The statement had fallen on quite unheeding ears in Cousin Jasper's case, but had been treasured up by the butler.

39

"Yes, I can drive it," agreed Oliver, rather doubting whether Cousin Jasper would really desire him as a chauffeur. He got up and went downstairs, to find his cousin waiting in the hall, so nervous and impatient that he made no other comment than:

"We must make haste."

Oliver hurried out to the garage, backed out the heavy car, paused under the portico for Cousin Jasper to climb in beside him, and sped away down the drive.

"Which way?" he asked, as they came out through the gate, and was directed along the road he had followed that afternoon.

"You may go as fast as you like, I am in a hurry," was Cousin Jasper's unexpected permission, so that Oliver, nothing loath, let out the car to its full speed. It was very dark, for the moon had gone under a cloud. The road, showing vaguely white through the blackness, was nearly empty and the tree trunks flashed by, looking unreal in the glare of the lamps, like the cardboard trees of a scene on the stage. The big car hummed and the wind sang in Oliver's ears, but for only the briefest moment, for they seemed to come immediately to a crossroad, where Cousin Jasper bade him turn. A slower pace was necessary here, for the going was rough and uneven, yet not so difficult as that of the narrower lane in which they presently found themselves. Here the machine lurched among the deep ruts, rustled through high grass and low-hanging trees, and finally came to a stop before a gate.

"No, wait here," directed Cousin Jasper as Oliver made a move to get out. "I shall not be gone very long."

He climbed out and jerked at the gate, which, one hinge being gone, opened reluctantly to let him pass. He stalked away, a tall, awkward figure in the brilliant shaft of light from the lamps, walking with a fierce, determined dignity up the path that disappeared into the dark.

Oliver felt a sudden rush of pity for him and of shame that he had so nearly deserted him.

"It must be hard," he thought, "to be so miserable and anxious, and to have no one to talk it over with. And I do wonder what is the matter?"

He waited an hour—and another. He had dimmed his lamps and could see vaguely the outline of a house, with one dull light in a window. A dog barked somewhere beyond the gate, and presently a child began crying. It cried a very long time, then at last was quiet, but still no one came. Oliver fell asleep finally against the comfortable leather cushions, and slumbered he knew not how long before he was aroused by the protesting creak of the broken gate. He thought, as he was waking, that a man's voice, high-pitched with anger, was talking in the dark, but when he had rubbed the sleep from his eyes, he saw no one but Cousin Jasper.

"I had not thought it would be so long," was all his cousin said as he got in, and after that there was no word spoken until they entered their own gate and rolled up to the door.

"You drive well for a boy. Good night," said Cousin Jasper as he climbed out and entered the house. In his hurried, awkward way, he was attempting to express his gratitude, but he had managed to say the wrong thing.

"For a boy, indeed," snorted Oliver, as he guided the car into the door of the garage, and repeated it as he went up the stairs to his room: "For a boy!"

The big clock in the hall was solemnly striking one.

Oliver was wondering, as he came down to breakfast next morning, what his cousin would say in explanation of their midnight expedition, but discovered that Cousin Jasper had adopted the simple expedient of saying nothing at all. The matter was not even referred to until just as they were leaving the table, and then only indirectly.

"I should have thought of it before," their host said, "that it might give you some pleasure to take out the car. Use it every day, if you wish, and take Jennings or not, just as it suits you. I have real confidence in your driving, Oliver."

It was surprising how completely matters were put upon another footing by what he had said. If Cousin Jasper had confidence in him, Oliver thought, he need no longer feel like a neglected outsider, one who was of no use or worth in the household.

"Get your hat, Janet," he urged promptly.

He had not an instant's hesitation in deciding where they would go first.

Just as Cousin Jasper was entering his study he turned back to say:

"Now about your Cousin Eleanor——".

But Oliver either did not or would not hear, as he sped away toward the garage. Perhaps Cousin Jasper understood the smile that Janet gave him, for he smiled himself and said no more.

In the very shortest time possible, Oliver and Janet were bowling along the smooth white road with all the blue and golden sunlight of a cool June morning about them. Oliver laughed when he thought of his dusty progress along that way the day before. There was little danger of his running away now, for the dreaded Cousin Eleanor was quite forgotten and he was certain that the time would not pass slowly since he had acquired this splendid new plaything.

He wondered, as the highway spun away beneath the swift wheels, which of the crossroads that he passed was the one that he had traveled the evening before, but the night had been so dark and their speed so great that he was quite unable to decide. It was only after exploring a good many of Medford Valley's lesser thoroughfares, after awkward turns in narrow byroads that proved to be mere blind alleys, that they began to come closer and closer to the foot of the hill. Not being able to find a

The Windy Hill

direct path, Oliver finally drew up beside the low stone wall and plunged, on foot, through the high grass of the orchard.

"Wait until I see if they are here," he instructed Janet, "and then I will come back for you."

His new acquaintances were sitting on the bench beside the doorway as he came up the hill, Polly in a very trim blue dress and without her apron, but the Beeman in his same dilapidated overalls. The girl had a notebook on her knee and was putting down records at her father's dictation.

"Here is our friend in need, of yesterday," said the Beeman cordially as Oliver came up the path, "but we can't put him to work to-day because we are just about to set off to fetch some new beehives. There are more colonies than I thought that need dividing, and I find I am out of hives."

"Let me get them for you," Oliver offered at once, and explained the presence of his sister in the car below.

"Polly can go with you to show you the way," the Beeman agreed willingly. "John Massey, who makes our hives for us, lives a good many miles away, at the upper end of Medford Valley. I shall be glad to save the time of going myself. Come to the top of the hill, so that I can point out the direction of the road to you."

They took the little path beyond the house, leading upward to the very summit of the hill. In the direction from which Oliver had come, up the gentler incline of the southern slope, the view was narrowed by the woods and the orchard, showing only the long vista that led away toward the high ridge opposite and the blue dip of shining sea. On the eastern face of the hill, however, the ground fell away steeply to a sweep of river and a broad stretch of green farming country. It lays below like a vast sunken garden, with great square fields for lawns and clumps of full-leaved, rounded trees for shrubbery. The yellow-green of wheat and the blue-green of oats stretched out, a smooth expanse that rippled and crinkled as the wind and the sweeping shadow of a cloud went slowly down the valley. There were no country houses of high-walled, steep-roofed magnificence here, only comfortable farm dwellings with wide eaves and generous barns, a few with picturesque, pointed silos and slim, high-towering windmills.

"Most of that farming land belongs to your Cousin Jasper," the Beeman said, while Oliver, too intent upon staring at the view below him, failed to wonder how he happened to know so much of their affairs. "That whole portion of the valley was waste, swampy ground at one time; it was an uncle of Jasper Peyton's who drained the land thirty years ago and built dikes to keep the river back. He arranged to rent it out to tenant farmers, for he said one man should own the whole to keep up the dikes and see that the stream did not come creeping in again. Medford River looks lazy and sleepy enough, but it can be a raging demon when the rains are heavy and the water comes up. Your cousin owns all of it still except for a portion up there at the bend of the stream. That has passed out of his hands lately. It is at the far end, on the last farm, that John Massey lives."

Oliver from this vantage point could pick out the intricate succession of lanes and highroad that he must take to cross the river and reach John Massey's place, showing from here as only a dot of a gray house at the angle of the stream. The sunshine was very clear and hot over the valley below, but the oak tree spread its broad shadow all about them and bowed its lofty head to a fresh, salt-laden wind.

"See how still the trees are along the river," said the Beeman, "but the oak tree is never quiet. The breeze comes past that gap in the hills, yonder where you can look through to the sea, and it seems never to stop blowing. So we call this place the Windy Hill."

The three set off on their errand very gayly in the big car, although Polly and Janet, in the back seat together, were a little shy and silent at the very first. At the end of a mile, however, they were beginning to warm toward each other and had set up a brisk chatter before they had gone three.

"I knew Janet would like Polly," Oliver was thinking. "She is the sort of girl I like myself, not like Cousin Eleanor. The kind that makes you feel that your clothes and your manners are all wrong and that you haven't anything to say—those are the girls I can't stand."

He quite forgot that this harsh judgment of his unknown relative was not based upon any real evidence.

When they reached the floor of the valley they found it as level as a table, with a straight road running from end to end, along which they sped in a whirling cloud of dust. Other cars passed them, driven by prosperous farmers, the growl and clatter of motor tractors sounded from the fields on either hand. Halfway up the valley the character of the places seemed to change, the houses had the look of needing paint, the weeds were taller along the fences, and there were no silos nor tractors to be seen. As they neared John Massey's house, the road came close to the river, with the high, grass-covered bank of earth that was the dike rising at their left as they drove along.

They were obliged to stop where some horses were walking in the road ahead of them and seemed slow in making way. The big gray and brown creatures were dragging huge flat stones, each hooked to the traces with an iron chain, scuffling and scraping along in the dust.

"I'm sorry," said the sunburned man who drove the last team, looking back to where the car waited in the road. "We'll make room in a minute, but the horses are doing all they can."

"We are in no hurry," responded Oliver. "Where are you taking the stones and what are they for?"

"To mend the dike, quite a way downstream. It takes a lot of patching to keep banks like these whole and strong, but they guard some valuable land. The dike looks as though it needed repairs up here at this end, but nobody does much to it. Mr. Peyton has us go over his section of the banks every year."

The horses moved forward, leaving room for them to pass, and the car went on.

John Massey's house was the last one at the end of the road, a little place with a roof that needed new shingles and with sagging steps leading up to the door. Oliver, with some difficulty, squeezed the big car through the gate and followed the rutty driveway to the open space behind the house. There was a stretch of grass, a well, two straggling apple trees, and a row of beehives. An inquisitive cow came to the gate of the barnyard and thrust her head over it to stare at them with the frank curiosity of a country lady who sees little of strangers.

"Here is John Massey," said Polly, as a rather heavy-faced, shabby man with kindly blue eyes came out of one of the barns. "My father gave him some of these beehives and taught him how to make new ones. He is very clever at it, and it means a good deal to him to make ours, for he is very poor. He works very hard on his farm, but it never seems to be much of a success."

The hives were brought out and paid for and stowed in the back of the car. Oliver was just making ready for the somewhat difficult feat of backing the car around in the narrow space between house and barn, when there came a rattling of wheels through the gate and a loud, rasping voice was heard calling for John Massey.

"That's Mr. Anthony Crawford," said the farmer, who had been standing by the car admiring wistfully its shining sides and heavy tires. "He owns this place and he comes up here nearly every day to see how I'm farming it. I don't accomplish much with him always around to give me sharp words and never a dollar for improvements. I've told him a hundred times that the dike ought to be looked after this year or we'll be having a flood, but he always says he guesses it will hold. Yes, sir, I'm coming."

The calls had grown too loud to be disregarded, although it was plain that John Massey was in no haste to obey the summons. In a moment the owner of the voice came jingling and rattling around the corner of the house, the same narrow-faced, gray-eyed man that Oliver had met on the road, driving the same bony, knock-kneed horse.

"Whoa, there, whoa!" cried the driver, for the old white steed had caught sight of the car and was testifying to its dislike of it by grotesque prancings and sidlings that threatened to wreck the ramshackle trap. "Here, get out of my way!" he ordered Oliver, "that is, if you know how to handle that snorting locomotive that you think you're driving."

Red with anger, Oliver started his engine and embarked upon a maneuver that was difficult at best, and, under the present unfavorable circumstances, proved to be nearly impossible. He turned the car half round, collided with a pigsty, backed into the barnyard fence, and narrowly missed taking a wheel off Anthony Crawford's decrepit wagon. That gentleman assisted the process with jeering remarks and criticisms, while Oliver grew redder and redder with fury and embarrassment. At last, however, the car was turned and stood for a moment in the driveway, facing the white horse which seemed to have resigned itself to the presence of the puffing monster and to be very reluctant to move.

"I have got out of your way, now will you be good enough to get out of mine?" said Oliver very slowly, lest the rage within him should break out into open insult.

In spite of his anger he could not help noticing that the man before him moved with a curious easy grace, and that when he smiled, with a white flash of teeth, he was almost attractive. It was impossible to deny that, except for his thin lips and his hard gray eyes, he was handsome.

"He must be about Cousin Jasper's age," Oliver thought as he sat looking at him while the other stared in return.

"I should like to pass," the boy persisted, since the other made no move.

"So you shall, Mr. Oliver Peyton," returned the man, "only don't expect me to move as fast or as gracefully as you did. You wonder how I know your name, I suppose. Well, if that precious Cousin Jasper of yours and mine were a little more outspoken about his affairs, you would know all about me. If you want to know where I live, just look over the back wall of your cousin's garden. Do it some time when he isn't looking, for he doesn't love to think of what lies behind that wall where the fruit trees are trained so prettily and where the trees and shrubs grow so high."

He had made way at last and the car moved forward, but he turned to shout a last bitter word after them.

"If you want to know one of your Cousin Jasper's meanest secrets, look over the wall."

CHAPTER IV.

THE GARDEN WALL

It was very early when Oliver rolled out of bed next day, sleepy but determined. He had decided, at first, to pay no attention to Anthony Crawford's suggestion, made evidently with malicious purpose; he had, indeed, almost forgotten it by the time he and Janet reached home. But Janet had remembered, and she had brought up the question that evening as they went up to their own quarters rather later than usual, since Cousin Jasper had been sitting with them in the library and had seemed unwilling that they should leave him.

"There is something very wrong in this house," declared Janet. "Hotchkiss doesn't know what it is, Mrs. Brown doesn't."

"I think the Beeman knows," Oliver volunteered suddenly, although he could give no reason for his guess.

"Anyway," pursued Janet, "some one ought to know, for some one ought to help Cousin Jasper. I am certain that he has no mean secrets, as Anthony Crawford said. And so I think one of us should climb up and look over the wall. It had better be you," she added wisely but regretfully, "because, if we both try it, some one is sure to see us."

It was, therefore, Oliver who was stirring at sunrise, for his investigations must be made before any one else was up. He let himself out of the house very quietly and crossed the empty, silent garden. He had forgotten how beautiful a garden could be in the early morning with the dew shining on every grass tip and with the flowers all radiant in the vividness of color of newly created things. There were gay-colored beds below the terrace and long borders at each side of the house, then a wide stretch of grass behind the garage, and beyond that, back of the shrubs and the fruit trees and the thickly growing vines, was the wall. It was higher than the boundaries at the sides and front of Cousin Jasper's place, perhaps to afford a better surface for the grapevines and pear trees trained against it, perhaps for another reason.

Oliver walked along it slowly, looking up at the smooth bricks and wondering how it was to be climbed. The more difficult it appeared the more determined he became to get to the top. In the middle of the wall behind a summerhouse stood a stout trellis, the support of an exceedingly thorny rose vine. Here, he decided, was the place to scramble up, but he must make haste, for people in the house would be waking and would see him. Carefully he set a foot upon the lowest bar, found that it would hold, and began mounting upward.

There were trees beyond the wall, not the trimmed, well-kept kind that grew in Cousin Jasper's garden, but a scrubby growth of box elder and silver-leaved poplar such as spring up in myriads where the grass is never cut. Hanging over the top of the coping, he could peer through their branches and see a house beyond. He was astonished to see the shingled roof rising so close by, for he had not thought that they had neighbors who dwelt so near.

The house was a square one of yellow stone, with overhanging eaves and small windows and an old-fashioned stoop in front, over which the roof came down in a long sweep. It must have been built a hundred years ago, he thought, and it might have seemed a charming, comfortable old place were it not so unutterably dejected and dingy. Its windows were cracked, the grass grew tall and ragged upon its lawns, a litter of rubbish lay about the back door, and the woodwork, that should have been white, was gray from want of paint.

"It looks as though the people who lived in it just—didn't care," Oliver commented. "It is a nice old house, but it seems worn out and discouraged, somehow, like John Massey's cottage. I wonder who owns it."

An open space between the dwelling and the wall had apparently once been a broad lawn, then had been plowed up for the planting of a patch of grain, and had at last been left as a neglected waste for weeds and brambles to flourish undisturbed. An old scarecrow still stood knee-deep in the tangled green, left there after the field had been abandoned, to drop slowly to pieces in the wind and rain. The grotesque figure, with its outstretched arms and hat set at a rakish angle, looked familiar for some incomprehensible reason. As Oliver clung to the wall, squinted through the leaves, and wondered why that should be, the mystery was suddenly solved. The door of the house opened with a squeak of rusty hinges and somebody came out on the step. It was Anthony Crawford. No wonder the scarecrow looked like its master, for it was wearing his old clothes, garments to which there always cling a vague resemblance to the person who once wore them.

A child with very yellow hair came running out upon the doorstone, laughing aloud at some small joke of his very own. When he saw Anthony Crawford, however, he sobered suddenly and slipped back into the house without a sound. The man stood upon the step and stared, with narrowed, penetrating eyes, over toward the wall. The gables and chimneys of Cousin Jasper's big house must show through the trees from where he stood and, judging by the look with which he regarded them, it seemed that he hated the very roof that sheltered Jasper Peyton. The luxurious mansion was, in truth, a sharp contrast to the unkempt, gone-to-seed yellow farmhouse, although Oliver wondered whether, originally, the old stone dwelling had not been the more attractive of the two.

He leaned forward to see plainer, made an unwise move, and attracted the attention of the man on the step. The boy flushed scarlet as their eyes met, for Anthony Crawford, without making a sound, went through a pantomime of an ecstasy of glee. He had evidently expected to arouse Oliver's curiosity by his suggestion the day before, and was overcome with ill-natured delight to catch him in the very act of satisfying it.

With a mutter of angry words, Oliver dropped back into the garden.

"I wasn't looking just because he told me to—I wasn't!" he kept repeating.

As he walked toward the house he looked back more than once at the high wall, wondering at the things it hid. Here was squalid poverty almost under the windows of the great, handsome house where Cousin Jasper lived with everything that heart could desire. It was the poverty, too, of a member of his own family. Here was jealous enmity also, a hatred that seemed to point ominously to trouble before them, to all the harm that could be accomplished by an angry, unscrupulous man. No wonder Cousin Jasper looked changed, and haunted. What hold did Anthony Crawford have upon his cousin; why should one have so little and the other so much; why did that high wall forbid all intercourse with that strange neighbor? It was plain to Oliver at last that their night ride through lanes and crossroads had been necessary because the wall cut off any direct path, and that the goal of their expedition in the dark had been Anthony Crawford's sagging, one-hinged gate.

The morning sun was rising higher, the cheerful sound of a grass cutter was going up and down the garden, and smoke was mounting from the kitchen chimney. With some care, lest he should be asked the cause of his scratched hands and torn sleeve, Oliver slipped into the house and sought his own room.

He and Janet talked over all that he had seen, but they could make little of it and were, indeed, more mystified than ever. At intervals during the day, they kept coming back to the subject and were still talking of it that evening as they sat in the library with the long windows open upon the terrace and upon the flowering garden. They had come to no conclusion, however, when the study door opened and Cousin Jasper came toward them across the hall. He looked less troubled to-night, and was smiling as though he had been looking forward to this hour they were to spend together. Yet his face changed in a moment at the sound of rattling wheels on the drive, followed by the appearance of a troubled Hotchkiss at the door, with the reluctant question:

"Will you see Mr. Crawford, sir?"

The visitor had not waited, but came pushing in behind him.

"We do not need to stand on ceremony," he said, "when it is all in the same family. These are your two guests, eh? You need not introduce them, we have met before. I saw the boy very recently, in fact; he seems to be an enterprising fellow and was conducting some investigations of his own. Well, well, we won't talk of it now."

Oliver writhed inwardly under his sharp glance, but could muster no appropriate reply. He was thinking again that Anthony Crawford might have been handsome except for those restless gray eyes that were set too near together. Although his host was obviously anxious to lead him away to the study, the visitor planted himself in the middle of the library floor and stood his ground firmly.

"Have you thought over my offer, Jasper?" he said. "Are you ready to give me my share, or shall I take all?"

"I have given up what seemed your share," Jasper Peyton returned steadily, "and rather than quarrel with you further I would gladly give you all. But I believe to shut one's eyes to justice is wrong, even in such a matter as this."

The other's calm broke suddenly under the force of ungovernable anger.

"You will be sorry," he cried. "You will lose more than those fat acres by the river and this fine house where you hoped to live so happily—until I came. You won't give in, will you? Your high principles—or your stubbornness—will still hold you back from giving me what is mine? Then I can tell you that I will drag your good name down where my own stands, I will publish that disgrace of mine that you hushed up to save the family pride. You will have people looking into your own past; they will be saying, 'If one of the family was crooked, why not another?' There is always a pack of gossips and scandalmongers who are only too glad to snap at the heels of any prominent man. I will loose them all upon you, Jasper Peyton, every one."

He stopped, perhaps to draw breath, while Cousin Jasper stood before him, very silent and very white. The man's narrow eyes turned first to Oliver who was bursting with unexpressed rage and then to Janet who was regarding him with astonished and horrified disapproval.

"You do not like my way of talking?" he said to her. "I assure you that all I have said is the truth."

"Then I should not think," she replied bluntly, "that you would have many friends if you often tell them the truth in just that way."

"I have no friends," he declared. "Friends exist only to hurt you; it is my belief that men prosper better alone. Have no illusions, trust nobody, feel that every man's hand is against you, and then you will know where you stand. That is my policy. Your soft-hearted cousin, here—his one mistake is that he trusts every one, he likes everybody. He even trusts me a little, on very small evidence, I can assure you. He would hate me if he could, but, because we are of the same blood, he cannot even bring himself to do that. Eh, Jasper, am I not right?"

"If you think you have said enough to these children," said Cousin Jasper, wincing, but still quiet, "perhaps we had better discuss this business further in some other room."

"Very well," returned the other, quite good-tempered again. "I should be glad enough to have them hear the whole. But of course if there are some things that you do not wish known——"

He walked away toward the study, quite at his ease, humming a tune and casting sharp, appraising glances about him as though the thought of ownership were already in his mind. The door beyond the hall closed behind them.

"What a hateful man!" cried Janet, almost in tears. "Poor Cousin Jasper! And we can't do anything to help him."

Oliver, equally miserable, stood at the window. The moon was coming up behind the trees, a great red moon just past the full, misshapen and lopsided, that seemed to be laughing at them. He stamped his foot in angry impotence.

"And he doesn't seem to me even to believe in himself; it is as though he were playing a part, just showing off." He pointed through the window at the disgraceful cart and dejected old horse standing before the wide white steps.

"I don't think he has to drive that wretched wagon at all. He just does it to make Cousin Jasper ridiculous."

The session in the study was prolonged so late that in the end Janet and Oliver abandoned their sleepy effort to wait until Anthony Crawford should depart, and went dispiritedly upstairs to bed.

"I have made up my mind to one thing," said Oliver firmly, as they reached the top of the stairs, "I am going to ask the Beeman what we ought to do. I feel as though I had known him always and I am sure he can help us."

"But ought we to tell him Cousin Jasper's secrets?" objected Janet doubtfully, "and, by the way, what is his name? You never told me."

"Why—I don't know it," exclaimed Oliver in a tone of complete astonishment. "I never even noticed that I didn't. It doesn't matter, I will ask him to-morrow. And you understand, from the first minute he speaks, that you can trust the Beeman."

He went away to his room where, so it seemed to him, he had been asleep a long time before the rattle of wheels aroused him. He peered drowsily through the window and saw the old white horse with its lean, erect driver move slowly down toward the gate, long-shadowed and unreal in the moonlight, fantastic omens of some unknown mischief that was brewing.

Next morning, as he and Janet left the car beside the orchard wall and climbed the grassy slope of the hill, Oliver's one misgiving was lest the Beeman should not be there. But yes, as they came up the steep path they heard voices and smelled the sharp, pleasant odor of wood smoke drifting down toward them. The wind was high to-day, singing and swooping about the hilltop, slamming the swinging door of the house, and scattering in all directions such bold bees as had ventured out to ride down the boisterous breeze to the honey-filled meadows below.

Janet was as warmly welcomed as Oliver, and they were both bidden to come in and sit down beside the table where Polly was sorting the little wooden boxes in which the bees build the honeycomb.

"We were just going to begin a story," said the Beeman. "Polly has been clamoring for it for half an hour."

"But I wanted to ask you something," broke in Oliver, too much excited for good manners. "Couldn't you wait?"

"I believe," said the Beeman slowly, giving him an odd glance that seemed to carry a message of complete understanding, "I believe that sometimes it is better, when you are troubled about something, to cool off and settle down, and come at an affair slowly. And I think this is one of the times."

Oliver nodded. He felt quite sure that the Beeman was right.

CHAPTER V.

THE GHOST SHIP

Cicely Hallowell sighed deeply as she pushed away the heap of papers before her and brushed back the hair from her aching forehead. She was weary of her task and the room was growing dark and cold. She was beginning, moreover, to be uneasily conscious that the two men at the far end of the long table had forgotten her presence behind the pile of great ledgers and were talking of things that she was not meant to hear.

Half an hour earlier her brother Alan had rushed in to see whether she were not ready for their afternoon ride and had been disappointedly impatient when she shook her head.

"It is a glorious day, so cold and the roads so deep in snow. The horses are like wild things, and will give us a famous gallop up the valley. Oh, do come, Cicely."

But no, she must stay in the big gloomy countinghouse, to finish the letters that she had promised to copy for her father, while Alan had flung off, saying over his shoulder, as he departed to take his ride alone:

"It is very wrong to miss fun and adventure by toiling and moiling here. Think how the sea will look and how the blasts will be blowing over our Windy Hill!"

The place seemed very cheerless and empty after he had gone. The long windows gave little light on that gray winter afternoon, and the big fireplace with its glowing logs was at the far end of the room. There were shadows already on the shelves of heavy ledgers lining the walls, and on the rows of ship's models all up and down the sides of the big countingroom. Those lines of dusty volumes held records that Alan was forever reading, tales of wonderful voyages, of spices and gold dust and jewels brought home from the Orient, of famines in far lands broken by the coming of American grain ships, of profits reckoned in ducats and doubloons and Spanish pieces of eight. Cicely was fond of drawing and loved, far more than copying dull letters, to make sketches of those miniature vessels in the glass cases that stood for the Hallowell ships that had scoured the oceans of the world. They had been wrecked on coral reefs in hot, distant seas, they had lain becalmed with priceless cargoes in pirate-infested waters, their crews were as skillful with the long guns as they were at handling the sails, their captains were as at home in Shanghai or Calcutta as they were in the streets of the little seaport town where they had been born. Cicely could remember when the big countingroom had been crowded with clerks and had hummed like a beehive with the myriad activities of the Hallowell trade. It was a dull and empty place now, and the fleet of Hallowell ships was scattered, some lying at anchor, some dismantled and sold, some fallen into the hands of the enemy. For this was the third year of that struggle with England that the histories were to call the War of 1812.

Cicely, for all her thirteen years, looked very small, sitting there at the end of the long table, in her "sprigged" high-waisted gown, her feet in their strapped slippers perched on the rung of the high office stool. She had just taken up her pen to begin writing again when the voices of the two men by the fire rose so suddenly that she dropped it, startled. Her father's tone fell almost immediately to strained quiet, but Martin Hallowell, his partner, went on with angry insistence. She knew him to be hot-headed and impetuous, but she had never heard such words from him before.

With a quick, eager motion that was the embodiment of impatient greed, Martin was running his finger down the columns of the ledger before him.

"There is no ship like a privateer, and no privateer like the Huntress," he was saying. "Send her on one more voyage and we shall be rich men."

There was an ugly tremor in his voice, that quavered and broke in spite of his attempts to keep it calm.

"I do not care to be one of those who gathers riches from a war," returned Reuben Hallowell, Cicely's father. There was something in the dry calm of his answer that seemed to stir Martin to uncontrollable anger.

"It is like you, Reuben Hallowell," he said, "to be willing to ruin my plans by your foolish scruples just when a real prize is within reach. But I vow you shall not do it. You shall be a wealthy man in spite of yourself, and let me remind you that, two years ago, before we built the Huntress, you were a precious poor one."

The Hallowell partners were not brothers, but cousins, with Cicely's father much the older of the two. They had inherited the business from their fathers, for such an ill-assorted pair would never have been joined together from choice. Many of their discussions ended in stormy words, but never before had Martin's dark face showed such white-hot, quivering rage as when he arose now, gathered up his papers, and went away to his own room, closing the door smartly behind him. Cicely got up also and went down the long countingroom to where her father sat by the fire.

"I heard what you and Cousin Martin were saying," she told him hesitatingly, "I am afraid you did not remember that I was there. But it does not matter, for I did not understand what Cousin Martin was so angry about."

"There is no reason why you should not understand," her father replied, rather slowly and wearily, she thought, "although sometimes I am not certain that I understand these troubled times myself. Across the seas the Emperor Napoleon, a long-nosed, short-bodied man of infinite genius for setting the world by the ears, has been warring with England for the last ten years and more. He and the British, with their blockades and embargoes and Orders in Council have long been striving to ruin each other, yet have achieved their greatest success in ruining a peaceable old gentleman in America who relies on his ships to bring him a livelihood. To oppress neutral shipping leads in the end to war, although I vow that often Congress must have felt that it should toss up a penny to determine whether the declaration should be against France or England. Some stubborn British minister, however, decided to countenance the stealing of sailors from our ships to fill up the scanty crews of their own navy, and a stubborn British nation felt that it must back him, so in the end the war was with England."

"And have we not won many glorious victories?" asked Cicely.

"Ay, there have been victories; out of her fleet of seven hundred and thirty sail, England has lost a handful to us and we have shown how small our navy is and how great is its spirit. There have been passages of arms on land, also, of which we do not love to talk. And we have sent out our privateer vessels, armed ships that prey upon England's commerce, yet do not belong to our navy. They have done great things, have cut deep into England's overseas trade, and have brought home many a valuable prize to fill the pockets of their owners. Such a vessel is our Huntress, built at your Cousin Martin's instigation and launched at the moment when our fortunes were at their lowest ebb. Since we had not sufficient funds to equip her, nearly every one in this town put money into her, from John Harwood the minister down to Jack Marvin who digs our garden. It was a patriotic venture and a risky one, but she has brought home great profits in prize money and our own share has reëstablished the firm of

Hallowell. Your Cousin Martin says that one more voyage will bring us not only profit, but real wealth. But I say," he struck his hand suddenly upon the table, "I say that there shall not be another."

"Why?" The question was startled from Cicely by his sudden vehemence, yet it was not from him that she was to receive the answer. The door opened to admit Martin Hallowell, who had come back, apparently, for a last word.

"You say," he began at once, "that the Huntress needs refitting and cannot be made seaworthy in less than a month?"

His partner nodded.

"I say that she shall sail in a week," declared Martin.

"And I say no," cried Reuben Hallowell.

"You say, too, that the war is nearly over, that the Peace Commission is sitting at Ghent, and that rumors are coming home that they are near to an agreement. That is your excuse for wishing to keep our privateers at home. You are a foolish and an overscrupulous man, Reuben Hallowell, for I say that such a reason makes all the more haste for her to be gone. We should reap what profit we can while there is yet time." He leaned forward, his dark, eager face close to theirs, all caution forgotten in the intensity of his purpose. "Once at sea the Huntress is beyond reach of tidings or orders. If she should take her last and richest prizes a little after peace has been declared, who will ever know it?"

He was silent and stood staring at them with unwavering, defiant eyes. Cicely could hear her sharply drawn breath as she waited for her father to answer.

"We are partners no longer, Martin Hallowell," he said. "We were not born to work together and it is clear that we have come to the parting of the ways. To-morrow we will make division of our holdings, for I tell you plainly that I will have no more to do with you and your dishonest schemes."

The Windy Hill

"It shall be as you say," Martin agreed, quick to press home an advantage. "And since it was I who urged the building and launching of the Huntress, it is only proper that she should fall to my share. She shall sail this day week, as I have told you. And you, my dear cousin, for your effort to stop her, shall soon be a most regretful man."

He went out, this time closing the door very gently behind him. The echoes of his vague threat seemed to hang in the great room long after he was gone.

"What—what can he do?" questioned Cicely.

Her father, with a visible effort, answered cheerfully, "An angry man loves to threaten, but we have naught to fear from him. And now," he gathered the big ledger under his arm, "I must work for a little in the countingroom and then we will go home."

Cicely, left alone, went back to fetch her letters and stopped for a moment at one of the long windows to look down upon the harbor where the Huntress dipped and swayed at anchor, a stately, beautiful thing that seemed to quiver with life as she rocked in the choppy seas, her shimmering reflection, beginning to be colored by the sunset, rocking and dancing with her.

"Oh, I must draw it," cried Cicely, catching up a sheet of fresh paper. "If only the light holds and the ship does not swing round with the tide!"

The minutes passed while she worked eagerly, but finally was forced to lay down her pencil, unable to see more in the dusk. The door flew open and some one came in with the impulsive rush that belonged only to her brother Alan.

"What, Cicely, still here and trying to draw in the dark? Let me see what you have done," he exclaimed. He lit a candle and examined the paper. "I vow, that is good. Oh, Cicely, that Huntress is a wonderful ship!"

For some reason there was a cold clutch at Cicely's heart.

"Yes?" she answered faintly.

"I have just had such a talk with Cousin Martin," the boy went on excitedly. "I did not quite understand the way of it, but he said that he and my father were to divide, and that the Huntress was to be his own, entire. He wants me to go with her on her next voyage. He says the war is not nearly done and that there will be many months of fighting and prize-taking still. He thinks a great fellow of sixteen like me should have been a ship's officer long ago, and I think so, too. What a good fellow Cousin Martin is!"

Alan admired his elder cousin greatly, Cicely well knew, and he had, indeed, a touch of the same excitable, headstrong nature. She could well understand how Martin Hallowell had dazzled the boy with tales of what he would see and do. Had there been such a plan in her cousin's mind when he first uttered his threat against her father? Or had it only flashed upon him as he met Alan running up the stairs, eager, vigorous, and ready for any adventure?

"It is all arranged," declared Alan, "except just to tell my father."

"No, no," she cried wildly, but he did not even listen.

"I will go in and speak to him now," he said. She could not even cry out as the door closed behind him.

Alan had his father's stern and steady pride, but there were differences of temperament that led to frequent clashes of will between them. Reuben Hallowell loved both his motherless children, but he understood his son less well than his daughter. What would be the result of that interview, Cicely wondered, sitting quaking beside the candle that burned so lonely in the gloom. Would her father know how to be firm and patient, how to undo the harm that Martin Hallowell had wrought? It seemed, as she sat there, shivering, that she could not endure the suspense.

She had not long to wait. The door banged open and Alan stood for a moment on the threshold.

"My father forbids my sailing on the Huntress. I have told him I should go in spite of him," he said.

He walked away along the corridor and down the stone steps, his feet quicker and lighter than Martin Hallowell's but his footsteps sounding, in some vague, terrible way, like his cousin's as he strode out and down the stairs.

Her father came in a moment later.

"You should have been at home long since this, my child," was all he said, and they went out together, without further talk of the matter, into the sharp air of the snowy night.

At the corner of the steep, narrow street, Cicely caught sight of Martin Hallowell talking to a man whom she recognized as an old seaman who had sailed for years upon the Hallowell ships. Something Martin had said must have angered the sailor, for he was talking loudly, regardless of who might hear.

"No," the old man was saying, "there's not every one in the world will do your bidding, though you may think so. You can defy the old one and talk over the young one to go your way, but there's one man will not sail on any ship of yours and that's Ben Barton. I'll starve ashore first."

Cicely's quick ear caught his words as she and her father passed by on the other side of the snow-muffled street. It did not seem that Reuben Hallowell had heard.

One day passed, two, three, four days, and Cicely's one thought was that the Huntress was to sail in seven. Workmen were swarming all over her like bees, hammering, calking, and painting, yet it was plain that they could not do in a week what needed a month to finish. Alan was at the wharf all day, holding frequent conferences with his cousin. Reuben Hallowell went to and fro among the townspeople, urging them to say that the ship in which they were part owners must abide at home. But either because they were less sure of peace than he, or because their eyes were blinded by past good fortune and hopes of future gain, they would not listen. Between father and son no words were passed, since each was waiting for the other's stubborn pride to give way.

On the fifth day Cicely had gone out to ride, on a clear, snowy afternoon, with the white world shining before her and with the highway iron-hard under the horses' feet. She missed Alan sorely, for this was their favorite road, up the valley to the west of the town, as far as the round bare hill with the single oak tree that they liked to call theirs. The servant with her had dropped behind, and she was just turning her horse into the bypath leading to the hill when she saw a sturdy figure coming down the slope. The brown face, tattooed hands, and the small bundle of possessions done up in a blue handkerchief could only be a sailor's, a sailor who proved to be Ben Barton.

"I'm going to the next seaport to find another berth, since I've refused to sail on the Huntress," he explained in answer to her questions. "Mr. Martin has had to get a new skipper and a new crew, for none of the old hands would sail when they heard it was against your father's wishes. There was a bark came in from Delaware to be laid up for repairs, with mostly Swedes aboard, and they have manned the Huntress from her. The ship is to sail on Friday at midnight, with the turning tide, but she goes without Ben Barton."

He dropped his voice and came nearer.

"I will tell you this—though I should not," he said. "There's some one to join at the last minute, who will get into a boat waiting at the wharf in the dark, some one you love, miss, who ought to be stopping ashore with the rest of us. You should find some way to keep him back."

"Oh, if I only could!" she cried.

"There's only you can do it," he answered. "Hallowell blood can only be ruled by Hallowell blood, as we say on Hallowell ships. Well, I'll be

The Windy Hill

going on again. I had climbed the path, there, to take one more look at the harbor, where you can see it between the hills. Maybe your father will find a place for me when his vessels go to sea for trade again, and I'll never forget him nor you, Miss Cicely. Do you remember how you and your brother once hid under the wharf, and called out from that echoing place as though you were lost souls out of the sea? There was one honest old sailorman that nearly lost his wits for terror, since we seafaring folk have no love for ghosts. Mark my words, there will no good come to the Huntress from setting sail of a Friday. For that alone I would stay ashore though there's other things to hold me, too."

He strode away down the snowy road, leaving Cicely, smiling at first at the recollection of that game that had so frightened him when she and her brother had played at ghosts, then grave in a moment when she thought how soon that brother was to be gone. On Friday, the day after to-morrow, he would sail unless she could stop him. But how could she?

The next day she made the desperate effort of appealing to her father, but quite in vain. Reuben Hallowell would not believe either that the Huntress would sail or that his son would go with her.

"And if Alan wishes to cut himself off from his own people forever, let him," he said finally, unable to endure the thought that any one should dare to defy his will. Friday came, the shadows of Friday night stole through the big house, yet nothing had been done.

Cicely sat by the fire in her chintz-hung bedroom, leaning back against the flowered cushion of the big armchair, gazing into the flames. In the next room she could hear vague sounds of Alan's preparations, feet going to and fro, a door opening and closing, a pair of heavy boots dropped upon the floor. The night was dark outside, with a blustering wind and occasional flurries of snow that struck sharply against the window.

It was ten o'clock. The sounds had ceased as though Alan had finished making ready and was waiting, perhaps sitting silent in the dark, perhaps lying down for an hour or two of sleep before the fateful hour of the high tide. Cicely heard her father, below, barring the door, putting out the candles, making ready for a night that would surely bring him no sleep. Presently he passed her door, glanced inside, and came in to stand for a minute beside her fire. How worn he had grown to look just within the space of this last week! He said scarcely a word; it was as though his unhappiness merely craved company and shrank from the knowledge of what the night might bring.

At last he said, "You should be in bed. Good night, my dear."

As he went out he turned to look back at her with a glance of haggard, helpless misery. It was as though he said:

"My pride has bound and stifled me. I cannot speak a word to stop him, but won't you, can't you, persuade him, somehow, not to go?"

Very carefully and without a sound, Cicely rose and went to her closet, to take down her warm fur cloak. She had realized, in the moment of seeing her father's pleading look, that she had a plan, one that had been in her mind ever since the day that she had talked with Ben Barton. What she had really lacked was courage to put it into execution. Yet now, as she drew the cloak about her and pulled down her hood, her hands did not even tremble, nor did her determination falter. The house was absolutely still as she stole noiselessly down the stairs and slipped out of the door.

For a girl who had almost never been allowed upon the street alone, the wintry night should have been full of terrors, but to Cicely they meant nothing. As she ran down the steep High Street with the gale blustering behind her, she saw things that she had never believed existed—a burly waterman quarreling with his wife behind a dirty lighted window, the open door of a tavern showing a candle-lit room with a crowd of shout-

The Windy Hill

ing sailors drinking within, a furtive black shadow that skulked into an alleyway and remained there, silent and hidden, as she passed.

She reached the wharves at last, where the wind was stronger and where the waves slapped and dashed against the barnacled piles, throwing their spray against the windows of the locked warehouses. Even now she did not hesitate. She ran, a gray, flitting form, across the open space at the head of the wharf and disappeared.

There was a wait of a few minutes, then came the dip of oars through the dark and the sound of men's voices talking above the high wind. Martin Hallowell was coming ashore in the boat that was to carry Alan away. Beyond them, the lights of the Huntress showed where she was getting up sail. Martin made the landing with some difficulty, climbed the ladder to the wharf, and stood bracing himself against the heavy wind.

"We are a little early," he said. "Hold fast there with the boat hook. He will be here in a——"

His voice was drowned by a strange sound, an unearthly wailing that seemed to rise from the water beneath, but which filled the air until there was no saying from what direction it came. It lifted and dropped, hung sobbing and echoing above the water, then died away.

"Holy St. Anthony help us!" cried the nearest sailor. "It is the soul of some poor drowned creature caught among the weeds."

"Give way," roared the man at the rudder, and with one accord the oars dropped into the water.

"Stop, wait! It—it is nothing, you fools," cried Martin Hallowell, but his own voice quavered with terror, and carried little reassurance to the frightened men.

The boat hung doubtfully a ship's length from the pier, the oars dipping to hold it into the wind, the men hesitating, ashamed of their terror yet fearing to come closer. Again the cry broke forth, resounding again and again, mingling in terrible, ghostly fashion with the splashing and gurgling of the water. The boat shot away into the dark, just as Alan came running down the wharf, shouting to them to come back. The sailors, however, bent to their oars, unheeding; the lantern in the stern dipped and jerked as they rowed away, and the light finally went out of sight as the boat drew alongside the Huntress. It was just possible to make out the big ship as she weighed anchor and, rolling and plunging, moved slowly out into the tideway.

"She's gone—without me!" cried Alan. "Oh, they might have come back, the cowards!"

"Did you hear that—that terrible sound?" asked Martin Hallowell. In a second's pause between the breaking of two waves, it was possible to hear his teeth chatter.

"Terrible!" cried Alan in disgust. "That was only my sister Cicely, hiding under the wharf. It was a game we once played to frighten Ben Barton. Come out," he ordered sternly, kneeling down and thrusting an arm into the dark space to help her.

Out Cicely came, wet and shivering, with her hair streaked with mud and her hands scratched and cut by the sharp barnacles. Her face showed white in the dark as she looked up appealingly at her brother, but he turned from her without a sign. Before she could follow him, Martin Hallowell had seized her by the arm.

"You?" he cried. "You?"

He shook her until she was dizzy, until the dark, windy world spun before her eyes, he cried out at her with a terrible voice and with words that she only half understood. All the rage stored up within him during his bitter struggle to get his ship under way, all the baffled hopes of his small-spirited revenge, all the shame for his recent terror broke forth into blind fury against the girl who had stood in his way.

The Windy Hill

"I will teach you," he shouted, grasping her arm tighter until she winced with pain, "I will show you that you can't——"

His words were cut short by a stinging blow across the mouth from which he staggered back, dropping Cicely's arm and staring in gaping astonishment at his assailant.

"That is my sister," said Alan, very stiff and quiet and suddenly very like his father. "Whatever she has done you are not to touch her. She has ruined my chance of sailing with the Huntress, but at least she has shown me what—what you are, Martin Hallowell."

With his arm about Cicely, Alan went down the pier, while Martin, confounded and silenced, stood staring after them. The two said nothing as they climbed the High Street, although much must have been passing in the boy's mind. As he pushed open their own door and came into the dusky hallway he spoke for the first time.

"Can you wait here by the fire a minute, Cicely? I am going up first to—to tell my father what a fool I have been."

The weeks of winter passed, news came that peace had been signed on Christmas Eve, one after another the ships of war came straggling home. Some had taken prizes, all had been harried by the winter storms—and none brought news of the Huntress. One Carolina vessel that put in for repairs told of picking up a crew adrift in boats and of setting them aboard a ship bound for Chesapeake Bay and the coast of Delaware.

"They were most of them Swedes," the sailors told Alan, "and they were not very willing to talk of the ship they had lost, but it might have been the Huntress."

Reuben Hallowell was straining all his resources to send his idle ships to sea and to reëstablish the trade of peace. Yet when he urged his fellow townsmen to strive to gain the commerce America had lost, lest it be gone forever, they still hung back.

"We must know first where we stand," they said. "There is hope still that we have not lost the Huntress and that she will come to port with fortune for us all."

A stormy February passed and there came at last a gusty day of March. It was a Sunday, with the air clean after a shower, and with all the townspeople moving down the High Street from their churches at the hour of noon. There had been a tempest of wind and rain, but it had cleared leaving the waters still gray but with the sky turning to blue. Cicely was among the first, walking with her father and brother, and had stopped, as they came to their own door, to glance down at the harbor laid out in a circle of moving blue water below them.

"Oh, look, look!" she cried suddenly.

A ship was sailing slowly up the bay, a stately ship that dipped a little and rose again as she came, but held her course steady for the wharves. Her sails shone white in the fitful sun, the lines of her hull showed dark against the gray water, the tracery of her rigging and even the colors of her flag were distinct against the sky, and yet—she did not seem like any ship they had ever seen before. Cicely having drawn that vessel, line for line, masts, hull, ropes, and spars, knew that this was the Huntress, yet what was so strange about her? Why was she so steady in those changing gusts of wind, what was there that made her sails so shining and transparent, like the texture of a cloud?

The girl was aware that, among the crowd that had gathered to watch the strange vision, Martin Hallowell was pushing to the front, gazing with all his eyes. Ben Barton, too, who had come back the week before, to ask for a place on Reuben Hallowell's ships, was pressing close to Alan's elbow.

"The wind's dead off shore and here she comes straight in," she heard the old sailor mutter. "Not even the Huntress could sail like that. And yet it is the Huntress right enough."

The Windy Hill

The vessel came nearer and nearer, then of a sudden stopped, quivered, as though struck by a violent adverse wind. Her main topsail blew out suddenly and went streaming forth in the gale, a jib split to ribbons before their eyes, and spar after spar was carried away. She careened, as though before a hurricane, her foremast came down with a soundless smother of sail and wreckage. Further and further she tilted, and then suddenly she had vanished and there was nothing left but the March sunshine and the tossing, empty bay.

The crowd stood breathless, waiting for some one to speak. It was only Ben Barton who was able to find his voice.

"I've heard of such things before," he said. "The wise skippers all say it is a mirage, but the wiser sailormen say it is a message from another world. She's gone, our Huntress is, and there's no wind under heaven will ever blow her home again."

Martin Hallowell had swung on his heel and was walking away down the street facing the fact, finally, that his venture was at an end. A tall man with dangling watch seals edged up to Cicely's father.

"I am satisfied at last, Reuben Hallowell, that our ship is lost," he said. "We did wrong to wait for war to make our fortunes, and it is high time that we went back to the lesser risks and the smaller gains of peace. Will you let me join in lading your next vessel? You are the only man among us who has known when a war ends and peace begins."

"I'm thinking there will be some tall ships sailing out of this port soon," said Ben Barton, speaking low to Cicely and Alan. "It will be on a better craft than the Huntress even that your brother will be officer before long. What seas we'll cruise, he and I, and what treasures we'll bring back to you, Miss Cicely. I'd go with the son of Reuben Hallowell to the ends of the earth—if only he never asks me to put to sea of a Friday!"

CHAPTER VI.

JANET'S ADVENTURE

Throughout the telling of the story, Polly and Janet had been very busy sorting and putting together the little honey boxes that were to be set in larger frames and hung in the upper story of the beehives. There was now such a great heap of them ready that the Beeman gathered them into a basket and, summoning Oliver to help him, carried them outside. He did not, immediately, go down the slope to the beehives, but set the basket on the step and sat down on the bench beside it.

"You had something to tell me," he said, "something that disturbed and excited you. I thought it might be better for you to wait a little. I should like to hear it now."

"Yes, it is clearer in my head now," Oliver agreed. "It is about my Cousin Jasper that we are visiting. I want to help him, though"—he smiled at the recollection, yet made frank confession—"that first day I was here I was so angry I almost hated him."

"If I thought that were true," responded his friend gravely, "I should have to ask you never to come here again, not only because I am fond of your cousin myself, but because I value my bees. There is an old superstition that you must not hate where bees are, for they feel it and pine away and die. I cannot have my bees destroyed."

The boy, looking up quickly at his broad, friendly smile, realized that the man believed neither the old superstition, nor that Oliver entertained any evil feelings.

The Windy Hill

"Perhaps," went on the Beeman, "the bees were in some danger that first day. You had it in mind, then, to go away for good, I think."

Oliver nodded. He wondered how he could ever have made that selfish resolution to run away.

"How did you know?" he asked.

"I had guessed it from—oh, various things. I am about the age of your Cousin Jasper, but I know more than he about people of your years from being Polly's father. I even had some idea of what was the immediate cause of your going." The boy flushed so guiltily that he went on, in kindly haste, "I am troubled about Jasper Peyton myself—yes, don't look surprised, I know him well enough to call him that. We all know one another in Medford Valley. I—I even work for him sometimes. Now tell me what you think is wrong."

Oliver, as he set forth his tale, had a feeling that not all of it was new to his listener, but he hearkened attentively to all that the boy had to say, frowning when he heard of Anthony Crawford's insistent and disagreeable visits.

"Your cousin doesn't know how to deal with a man like that," he commented. "He is too upright himself to know the mean, small, underhand ways that such a person will take to get what he wants. I know Anthony Crawford, too, and what he is trying to accomplish. It will take all of us, every one, to beat him. But we will, Oliver, I vow we will."

"What can we do, what can I do?" the boy persisted. He felt ready to accomplish great things at once. "And can't you explain to me what it is all about?"

To his great disappointment, the other shook his head.

"I feel that if your cousin does not wish to tell you himself, I ought not to," he said, "though I should like you to know. But there are two things that you can do. One is not to be impatient with your cousin when he makes tactless mistakes about—about how you are to be entertained. He depends on you and Janet for a little cheerfulness in his house."

"That isn't much to do," observed Oliver. "I hope the other is more."

"It is only this. To borrow a boat from John Massey—can you manage a sailboat? Good, I thought you looked like the sort of boy who could—and take a cruise up and down Medford River where it skirts that level farming land in the valley. I want you to bring me word of how the dikes are holding. You may not see what bearing that has upon the matter, but I assure you it means a great deal. Anthony Crawford thinks that he is a very clever man, but he is preparing a pitfall for himself, unless I am very much mistaken. And you and I may be at hand to see him tumble into it. The only thing is to see that he doesn't harm others as well as himself."

Oliver had one more question to ask.

"I want to know your last name, and Polly's," he said. "I can't think how you knew mine and I had quite forgotten to wonder about yours until Janet reminded me that I had never heard it. I have no name for you but the Beeman."

"If you want a longer name for Polly, you can call her Polly Marshall," his friend answered, "but as for me I rather like being called the Beeman. We will keep to that title a little longer if you are willing. And now it is high time that I gave some attention to my bees."

Oliver had no difficulty, later in the day, in borrowing the sailboat from John Massey, although he was obliged to give the vague message, "that man who keeps bees up the hill said you would lend her to me."

"Sure, I will," replied John Massey heartily. "Just be careful you don't go aground on the bars. The river is shallow for this time of year, though it can be pretty fierce when the floods are up."

Oliver shook out the shabby sail, set the rudder for a long tack downstream, and was off. The breeze was coming in gentle puffs, so that the boat moved slowly through the water, the ripples making a sleepy whisper under the bow and the tiller, now and then, jerking lazily under his hand. One side of the stream was marshy so that he pushed into tall grass and cat-tails and startled an indignant kingfisher who was dozing on a dead tree. The bird went skimming off, a flash of blue and white that he followed as he came about.

On the other side, the current ran close beside the high banks of earth that protected the fields within. The channel was scoured deep and the restless stream was cutting into the dikes, washing long black scars just above the water line.

"That oughtn't to be," pronounced Oliver, and was glad to see that, farther downstream, the carving away of the earth had been stopped by patches of broken stone. For at least a mile, however, at the bend of the river, the banks were crumbling and neglected.

He could look up and see, first the farms of the low-lying land, the treetops and pointed silos just showing above the dike, then the hillside, with the wavering white line of the road, then that strange, shabby dwelling of yellow stone almost hidden in its cluster of trees. Above it showed Cousin Jasper's house, very big and red, set upon the slope almost at the top of the ridge. On the other side of the stream there were fewer dwellings, the wooded slope rising to the more open green of the orchard and then to the grassy declivity of the Windy Hill. As he neared the bridge he passed a long gray stone house with its gardens a glowing mass of color that came down to the water's very edge. This, he remembered, was the abode of Cousin Eleanor, and he laughed at himself as, even at this safe distance, he steered his course very cautiously along the opposite bank.

At the bridge he was obliged to turn, and run before the wind to make his way upstream again. He lay stretched out comfortably along the rail, paying little attention to the boat and thinking of many things. There was Cousin Jasper—how Oliver had misjudged him that day he thought of running away. His cousin had been tactless and stubborn, but the Cousin Eleanor affair had been well meant, after all.

"I'll never meet her, though. I won't give in," he declared, almost aloud, and realized, in a breath, that his persistence and Cousin Jasper's were both cut from the same piece.

"I'm sorry for him and I'll help him," he told himself, "and perhaps he will learn something about boys after a while."

And there was Anthony Crawford! He flushed again as he thought of the man's gleeful delight when he had caught him looking over the wall. What power could he have, and what was the disgrace of which he had spoken? The Beeman was almost as mysterious as the others also; he had certainly managed to evade the question when Oliver had asked his name.

"The only one that there isn't a mystery about is Polly," he declared as he came to John Massey's little landing and rounded with a sweep to the boat's mooring.

Meanwhile Janet, who had been left to her own devices, had stumbled into an adventure of her own. She had made ready to go with her brother, but Cousin Jasper had called her to look at some new roses and had delayed her so long that the impatient Oliver had finally gone without her. When Cousin Jasper had returned to the house, she wandered rather disconsolately up and down the hedged paths and, finally coming to the big gate, she stood looking out. The road stretched away invitingly across the hillsides, the sleepy stillness of the afternoon was broken only by the occasional drone of a motor and by the grinding wheels of a big hay wagon that labored along the highway in the dust.

She walked out along the road, thinking that she would find a vantage point to look down to the river and see how Oliver was faring. The

The Windy Hill

way presently crossed an open ridge whence she could see the smooth stream and the sail creeping slowly out from the green shore. For some time she stood watching its progress, wishing vainly that she might have gone, until she became suddenly aware that some one was staring at her. Turning, she saw that a child with very yellow hair and very round blue eyes was sitting between two alder bushes on the edge of a ditch, gazing at her intently.

"What are you doing?" she asked, astonished, for the youngster, a square little boy of four or five years old, seemed far too small to be on the road alone.

"I was wishing I could go home," he answered.

There was a slight quivering of his chin as he spoke, as though the problem was rather a desperate one, but he was determined not to cry. "I was wishing on that hay wagon when it went by," he explained sedately. "I shut my eyes so I wouldn't see it again and break the luck, and when I opened them, you were there."

He climbed over the ditch and came to her side to tuck his hand confidently into hers. There seemed to be no doubt in his mind that she would take him home.

"Can you show me where you live?" she asked as they went along together.

"Oh, yes," he answered cheerfully. "There was a cow eating beside the road, and I passed it once, but it looked at me so hard when I went by that I was afraid to go back. I'll show you."

They walked along for some distance, he tramping sturdily by her side and chattering contentedly, giving her all sorts of miscellaneous and unsought information, that his name was Martin, that he had a little brother, that the brother was crying when he went away from home, that his mother was crying a little, too, that they had a red calf in the barn, and that there was a scarecrow in the field beside their house. He led her into a crossroad, then down a narrow, shady lane, where, as he had said, there was a mannerly old black cow grazing beside the way, who came to the end of her tether rope to greet them.

"I'm not afraid with you here," young Martin asserted boldly, and was even persuaded to pat the smooth black and white face of the friendly creature while Janet fed her a handful of clover.

When they reached a broken-hinged gate at the end of the lane, the girl began to realize that she was coming to the same place that Oliver had described to her. She stopped, feeling that she would rather not go on, but the little boy tugged at her hand.

"My father isn't here," he told her, as though some unhappy knowledge of his father's character made him understand her hesitation, "and my mother's crying."

With some reluctance, Janet pushed open the gate and went in.

A faded, shabbily dressed woman sat on one of the unpainted benches of the shady stoop, holding a baby in her arms. As Martin had said, slow tears of helpless misery were rolling down her cheeks, while from the bundle that she held came the worn-out, tired wail of a sick child.

"I don't know much, but I would like to help you," Janet said, sitting down beside her, while the woman choked with a fresh gush of tears at the unexpected offer of aid and sympathy.

"I don't dare put the baby down, he cries so," she managed to say at last. "Could you go into the kitchen and heat some water and bring out the blanket that I hung up to warm? I don't doubt the fire is out by now, but I haven't been able to move for fear he would begin choking again. Do you think you can manage?"

Janet managed very well, with Martin trotting at her heels to tell her where things could be found. She heated the water, warmed the blankets, and even rummaged out the tea caddy and brewed a cup of hot tea for the weary mother.

"You are a real blessing, my dear," said the woman as she put down the empty cup. "This boy has been sick with croup all night and I had quite forgotten that I had no breakfast."

"Has his father gone for the doctor?" Janet asked, as she brought out a cushion for the baby, who seemed to be quieter now and almost ready to drop asleep.

"No," replied the woman briefly.

She offered no explanation. It was evidently not a thing to be expected that Anthony Crawford should take an interest in an ailing child.

As Janet went back and forth, she was struck by the surprising charm that the old house showed within, quite out of keeping with its littered door-yard and outward disrepair. The white woodwork had gone long unpainted, it was true, and the floors were worn and uneven, but there was an airy spaciousness in the rooms, a comfortable dignity in the old mahogany furniture, and the grace of real beauty in the curved white staircase with its dark, polished rail. Everything was spotlessly clean, from the faded rag rugs to the cracked panes of the windows. The kitchen was, to her, the place of chief delight, for it ran all across the back of the house, with a row of low windows wreathed in ivy and commanding a wide view across the meadow lands beside the river. There was a modern cooking stove at one end of the room, a cheap, hideous, ineffective affair, but at the other was still the old fireplace, with its swinging crane, its warming cupboards, and its broad, stone-flagged hearth.

The baby was so much better that his mother was actually able to smile and to lean back contentedly in the corner of the bench.

"He is better off out here in the air," she said. "I believe he will be able to sleep in a little while. Now if I just had a strip of flannel to wrap around his chest! You would have to go up into the garret to look for it, and maybe rummage in one or two of the boxes. But I believe there should be some in the big cedar chest back under the eaves."

Guided by the faithful Martin, Janet climbed the stairs to the garret, where, in the warm, dusty air that smelled of hot shingles and lavender, she went poking about, seeking the roll of flannel that Mrs. Crawford assured her was there. She could find everything else in the world—old clocks, spindle-legged chairs, a high-backed, mahogany sofa, and a spinning wheel. At last she discovered what she needed in a box far under the eaves, but in pulling it out so that she could raise the lid, she knocked down a row of pictures that leaned against it. She bent to pick them up and set them in order again, then stopped to stare at them with a gasp of delighted astonishment.

Janet loved beautiful things, especially pictures, and she could be sure, at one glance, that these were pictures such as one does not often see. She remembered being taken by her father to a famous gallery to see a landscape so much akin to the one before her that they had undoubtedly been painted by the same artist, a green hillside with sailing clouds above it, on a clear October day, "the sort that makes you feel that you can see a hundred miles," as Janet put it. There was another, a winding white road running up a wind-swept valley with the trees bowing to a storm and a spatter of rain slanting across the hill, there was a portrait of a fierce old lady and another of a man with lace ruffles and a satin coat. There was a long, cool wave, breaking upon a beach where the whiteness of the sun-splashed sand was so vivid as almost to hurt her eyes.

She set them out in a row against the eaves and sat back on her heels to look her fill. Such pictures, to be gathered here in the dusty attic, to crack and warp and fade into ruin! She could not understand how they could have come there, nor did she spend much thought in wondering, so lost was she in that pure delight that the sight of truly beautiful things can bring. An old print with a cracked glass and broken frame caught her attention almost the last of all. It showed a ship, a tall frigate, under full sail, and had all the quaint primness of the pictures of a hundred years ago. The group of people supposed to be standing on the wharf was composed of gentlemen in very tight trousers and ladies with very sloping shoulders and absurd, tiny parasols. The vessel floated on impossible scalloped billows, but no old-fashioned stiffness could disguise the free beauty of the ship's lines and the grace of her curving sails. Her name was inscribed in faded gold letters below—"The Huntress, 1813." The Beeman's tale was still so vivid in her mind that there was no need for her to wonder where she had heard that name before.

"Why, it was a real story," she exclaimed, "and I thought he was only making it up!"

As she moved the print to a better light, a smaller picture, almost lost among the rest, fell down between two frames and rolled across the floor. She took it up and saw that it was a miniature, painted on ivory and framed in gold, the portrait of a young girl with high-piled brown hair and eager, smiling eyes.

"It looks like Polly," Janet thought, "but it could not really be a picture of her."

She turned it over and found the single name engraved on the back, "Cicely, æt. 17."

"Martin," she cried in the sudden inspiration of discovery, "Martin, come here quickly and tell me what is your whole name."

The little boy came out from a far corner where he had been examining dusty treasures on his own account and stood for a minute just where a beam of slanting sunlight dropped through the tiny window under the roof.

"Martin Hallowell Crawford," he said.

She would always remember just how he looked, standing there with the sunshine on his yellow mop of curly hair, his chubby face smiling and then whitening suddenly as they both heard a sound behind them. She turned to see Anthony Crawford standing upon the stair.

CHAPTER VII.

THE PORTRAIT OF CICELY

If Janet had needed any further clue to Anthony Crawford's character, she would have had it in the sudden trembling terror of his little son. She was shaking herself, yet she mustered an outward appearance of courage for a moment, as she turned to face him squarely and to hear his biting words:

"First the brother, peering over the wall, then the sister, rummaging through my house. Did Jasper Peyton send you here to find where I kept the picture of Cicely Hallowell that he was so reluctant to give up to me?"

"I didn't know it was Cicely Hallowell," returned Janet, trying to speak steadily. "I didn't even know that she was a real person; I thought she was just some one in a story."

Then as Crawford stepped nearer, as little Martin gave a sudden squeak of alarm, blind panic took possession of her. She ran toward the stairs and, though the man put out his arm to intercept her, she dodged under it with undignified agility and plunged down the steps. They were of the broad, shallow kind that made her feel, for all her speed, that she would never reach the bottom, yet she came at last into the hall below and out upon the stoop. She fled past Mrs. Crawford, sitting with the sleeping baby across her lap and looking up anxiously, with good cause for misgiving since she had heard her husband go up the stair.

It was only when she was safely outside the gate that Janet stopped to draw breath, to realize how her knees were trembling and how her heart was pounding. Yet it stopped suddenly and seemed to miss a beat when she realized something further, that she still held in her hand the miniature of Cicely Hallowell.

"Can I go back?" she wondered desperately, but knew instantly that she could never find courage to do so. She went on, hurrying and stumbling as she made her way down the lane. Only once she ventured to look over her shoulder and saw Anthony Crawford standing on the doorstep staring after her while the scarecrow that was so vaguely like him seemed to be lifting its straw-filled arm in a mocking gesture of farewell.

Janet and Oliver held an anxious conference that evening as they sat on the terrace, for until that moment they had not been alone together. She brought out the miniature and told of the astonishing and disturbing manner in which it had come into her possession, while Oliver wondered, in frank dismay, how it was to be restored to its owner.

"I can't think how I came to carry it away with me," wailed Janet. "Of course it was clutched tight in my hand and I was so frightened that I didn't think of anything but getting away. I thought of putting it down on the grass by the gate, but it is too valuable to risk being lost like that. And that man will say I stole it. I don't know what to do."

"We shall have to give it back to him," said Oliver firmly. "To-morrow we will——" but he stopped in the middle of his sentence, unable, even in imagination, to contemplate facing Anthony Crawford and giving him the miniature.

"Shall we tell Cousin Jasper?" Janet suggested, but Oliver declared against it.

"Anthony Crawford will be quite ready to say that Cousin Jasper sent you to get it from him. The miniature and the pictures seem to be part of the trouble, though I don't understand why. So if that man comes here with such an accusation, it would be better for Cousin Jasper to be able to say he knew nothing about it."

"Yes," assented Janet. "I believe, if he knew, Cousin Jasper would try to shield us and Anthony Crawford would use it as one more thing to hold over him. I am beginning to understand both of them better. We—we have overlooked a good many things about Cousin Jasper."

It was only a few minutes later that Cousin Jasper joined them, nor had he yet sat down in the long wicker chair that Oliver placed for him, before Hotchkiss came out with a message.

"John Massey is in the kitchen, sir, and he says to tell you that he would like to see you about something important."

"Bring him out here," Cousin Jasper directed, and, when the somewhat embarrassed visitor in his worn best clothes appeared upon the terrace he got up with as elaborate courtesy as he would have accorded the most distinguished guest.

"What is it, John?" he asked, for the sunburned farmer was evidently an old acquaintance. The other burst out with his news and his errand at once.

"I've been turned off, sir," he said. "Told to leave the farm, with no notice at all and my crops all in the ground. I'll admit I'm a little behind on my rent, but not many landlords around here collect as closely as Mr. Crawford does; they get all their money at the end of the season and don't haggle over it month by month when the farmer has nothing coming in. And what can you do on land that's never improved? He lets the place run down and then turns me out because I can't make a fortune for him on it. I—I was wondering if you couldn't do something for me, sir."

"Do something for you?" echoed Jasper Peyton. "I can't use any influence with Anthony Crawford, if that is what you wish."

"I don't understand it," the man persisted. "Three years ago you were my landlord and none of us ever had dealings with Anthony Crawford except that we used to know him when he was a boy. The whole bottom land along the river was yours and all your tenants were farming it for a fair rent and every one was satisfied. But then—he comes, and the upper half is his, we hear, and it is bad luck for us, as we soon know. Everything runs down, no one is treated fairly, and here I am, turned off at a word, and all his doing. Couldn't you make room for me farther down the river somewhere, sir, where the land is yours?"

He looked so red and anxious and unhappy that Janet's heart was fairly wrung for him. His wife was ailing, she knew, the season was backward, and here he stood, facing the loss of all his work and the necessity of beginning all over again. She waited eagerly to hear what offer Cousin Jasper would make.

"I—I can't help you, John," he said at last, very slowly and heavily. "Even if I made room for you on one of the lower farms, it would only stir up trouble, and you might wake up some day to find that Anthony Crawford was your landlord again, after all. I can give you the money to pay your rent, if you wish to stay where you are, but that is all that I can do. There are times when we are none of us free agents, or masters of our own affairs."

"I don't care to stay on, sir," John Massey returned. "I've had too many words with Anthony Crawford for things ever to go easy again. I've been patching up the dike with my own spare time, and maybe the farm has suffered by my doing it; anyway he says so and calls me a fool. I thought perhaps you would help me, since I'd been your tenant so long before he came." His voice, dragging with disappointment, trailed lower and lower. "I don't seem to know just where to turn. Well, good night to you, sir." He turned and walked heavily away.

They sat very silent after he was gone. Oliver was leaning against the terrace rail, Janet in her big chair was clenching her hands in her lap, Cousin Jasper, with his hands on the railing, stood in absolute quiet, staring out over the garden. The light of the house came through the long windows, falling on his face that was so pale and tired. He had seemed weary and unhappy for some time, but to-night he looked desperate. The minutes passed, but still he stood in silence, staring straight before him.

The sight of his distress seemed more than either of the two could bear. Oliver could think of nothing to say, but stood dumbly helpless, while Janet moved closer to their cousin and spoke with shy hesitation:

"Couldn't we help you? Won't you tell us what you are thinking?"

"I was only thinking," Cousin Jasper answered very slowly, "I was wondering, as I do sometimes lately, how strangely life can change and twist itself and make things seem other than they should be. If you have lived all your years following your own sense of honor, if you have tried, in everything you do, to be fair and just, how can it be, when the years have passed, that suddenly all the results of honest dealing should be swept away? How can it be that a man who has disgraced himself, whose ways are known to be everything that is devious and unfair, how can he gain power over you, threaten to take from you everything that is yours, even say that he can destroy your good name? How can every effort you make toward a fair settlement only render matters worse? Is there really something so wrong with the world that a dishonest man can work more harm than a man of honor can ever undo? Do you think so?" he concluded, turning to regard them from under his knitted brows as if he must, in his distress, find some word of reassurance somewhere.

"No," said Oliver emphatically, finding his voice somewhat to his own surprise. "I don't think so at all. I believe a man who does dishonorable things can—can mix you up and make you miserable, but he can't go on forever. His plans are bound to come to grief in the end."

His halting words carried the real earnestness of conviction. They seemed to give Cousin Jasper some sort of comfort, for his face relaxed, he moved from his tense attitude, and turned to walk up and down the terrace through the patches of light and shadow that lay between the windows. Janet thrust a friendly, affectionate hand under his arm as she walked beside him. It was a hot night, at June's very highest tide, with the garden at the summit of its beauty. The Madonna lilies were in bloom, showing ghostly white through the dark, rows and ranks and armies of them all up and down the walks and borders, sending sudden ripples of sweetness upward to the terrace whenever the faint breeze stirred. There was no moon yet, but the stars were thick overhead, and the moving lanterns of the fireflies glimmered among the trees, low down still as they always are in the first hours of the dark. Janet was thinking that when the world was so beautiful, it was difficult to believe that things could go entirely wrong in it, but she did not find it possible to put her idea into words. It may have been that Cousin Jasper was thinking the same thing as he stopped and stood for a long time at the head of the brick-paved stair leading down from the end of the terrace into the garden. At last he began to descend slowly, unable to make out the steps in the dark, so that he put his hand on her shoulder to steady himself. He spoke very suddenly.

"It is not only in body but in spirit that the old must sometimes lean upon the young," he said, and then, with his voice quite cheerful again, began to talk of how well the flowers were doing this year.

Oliver had followed them to the top of the stair and stood above them, listening, but not, apparently, to what Cousin Jasper was saying. His head was bent and he was straining every nerve to hear some far-off sound. His face looked troubled, then cleared suddenly as he came down the steps.

"Cousin Jasper," he said, "didn't I tell you that the gardener wanted you to know that the night-blooming cereus is open just now? Suppose we walk out to the back of the garden and see it."

His cousin hesitated.

"It is rather late," he answered. "It will be open still to-morrow night."

"Janet has never seen one," persisted Oliver, putting a firm arm through Cousin Jasper's, "and it might rain or something to-morrow night. She would be so disappointed and so would the gardener."

They went down the last steps together, into the sea of white lilies and drifting fragrance, and disappeared into the darkness toward the back of the garden.

In spite of his insistence, Oliver did not seem so deeply interested as the others in the plant that was slowly opening its pink flowers that have so brief and beautiful a season. The gardener, hastily summoned, came across the lawn to exhibit his favorite plant with the greatest pride, but Oliver left the others to admire and ask questions and, in ten minutes, came back alone. Coming upon the terrace again, he saw Hotchkiss, just inside the long window, ushering out a visitor who was talking in loud, easily recognizable tones.

"No, he doesn't seem to be here," Anthony Crawford was saying, "though I didn't believe you, until you let me come in and see for myself. I had something of great importance to say to him—and to the girl. Well, I will come again to-morrow."

He passed down the room and must have come very close to the light, for his shadow loomed suddenly, misshapen and bulky, all across the library, even dropping its black length over the terrace outside. It followed him, a striding giant, from window to window and then dwindled suddenly again as Anthony Crawford himself stood under the light in the doorway giving Hotchkiss final directions.

"Be sure to tell him that I shall be here to-morrow night and that I shall expect him to be at home," he ordered, then climbed into the creaking cart and drove away.

Hotchkiss stood peering into the dark after him, evidently sending no good wishes to speed him homeward. Seeing Oliver coming up the steps at the far end of the terrace, he walked down to speak to him.

"There was something more than usual wrong to-night," he said anxiously. "He vowed that he must see Mr. Peyton and didn't want to take my word for it that he was out. It was fortunate that he had gone into the garden."

"Yes," responded Oliver, "I thought I heard that miserable rattletrap turning in at the gate and I remembered, all of a sudden, that the gardener told me yesterday about the night-blooming cereus. I—I thought they ought to look at it at once."

Hotchkiss had been nervous and agitated during what must have been a stormy interview, and he found this sudden relief too great for the composure even of a butler. He burst into a great laugh of delight and slapped his knee in ecstasy.

"That was the way to serve him!" he cried. "To think that prying scoundrel found some one that was too clever for him, for once."

Oliver grinned broadly, but recovered himself in a moment.

"Hotchkiss," he said with great gravity, "you would never do for the movies."

Janet was eating her breakfast very deliberately next morning, lingering even after Cousin Jasper had left them and while Oliver sat back in his chair fidgeting in frank impatience. When her brother finally urged her to make haste she broke forth into an explanation that was almost a wail.

"It is because I can't forget where we have to go to-day," she declared. "Oh, why—why did I make such a terrible mistake and carry that miserable picture away?"

The Windy Hill

Even Oliver looked none too cheerful at the prospect before them.

"We have to do it," he agreed, "but I think we will go over to the Windy Hill first. I promised Polly's father I would tell him what I saw from the boat. But after that there will be plenty of time and we will go to Anthony Crawford's."

"I ought to go alone," Janet said, "for it was I who made the trouble. And shall we tell the Beeman?"

"Not until afterward," replied Oliver. "If there is difficulty about the picture it would be easier if no one were concerned but just ourselves. And indeed you won't go alone! We are in this thing together."

It had rained in the night so heavily that the clumps of larkspur and more tender plants were beaten down and only the shower-loving lilies lifted their wet, shining faces above the green. The sky was still overcast, with threats of another downpour, yet the two put on their raincoats and set forth undeterred.

"There is an old apple shed in the corner of the orchard where we can leave the car," said Oliver. "Polly showed me, last time, where we could drive in."

The highway was smooth and wet and the river was perceptibly higher under the bridge. They pressed onward, up the grass-covered road, drove through the gap in the orchard wall, and felt their way along the open lane between the apple trees. The car was finally housed in the shelter of the shed and Janet and Oliver raced up the hill, for the first drops of a new shower were just beginning to fall, and Polly, in the doorway of the cottage, was beckoning them to make haste. The downpour was a sharp one that pattered on the roof, ran streaming from the eaves, and blotted out the hills opposite. The grass and the orchard, however, seemed to grow greener every moment under the refreshing rain, and the clumps of pink hollyhocks that crowded about the doorstep lifted their heads gratefully.

"We can't do much with the bees for an hour or two," observed the Beeman, sitting down in the corner with his pipe. "Now tell me what you saw on the river, Oliver. I noticed your sail and knew that you were out."

Oliver made his report upon the scouring banks while the Beeman listened and nodded gravely.

"That is something we must look into," he declared. "It is like Anthony to have let things go. And now, if you have time to wait, suppose we have a story."

They had ample time, they assured him, being only too glad to postpone the errand that must come later. They were eager for another tale, moreover, for they were beginning to realize that these were not mere haphazard narratives, but stories with some definite bearing upon the places and people about them.

"We have plenty of time," Oliver assured him. "We are in no hurry at all. You might even make it a very long one."

The Beeman nodded assent with that queer smile that seemed to betray an uncanny understanding of the whole situation.

"A long one it shall be," he agreed, "for I have a good deal to tell you."

CHAPTER VIII.

THE FIDDLER OF APPLE TREE LANE

People said that the Brighton children could "never manage," when it was said that they were planning to live in the little cottage on the hill above Medford Valley.

"There's always a wind there from the sea, dearie," said old Granny Fullerton to Barbara Brighton. "It will search out your very bones, come winter."

Barbara shook her head cheerfully. A plump and rosy young person of twelve years old does not worry much about cold winds.

People said also, with the strange blindness of those who can live close by for years and yet never know what is in their neighbors' hearts, that it was an odd thing that Howard Brighton should have built that little house so far from the town in the midst of that great stretch of wild land where so few folk lived.

"It is marshy in the valley and wooded on the hills," Granny Fullerton said to Barbara, "with never a neighbor for miles. Of course the land has been in your family time out of mind, but those that are your nearest kin have always lived in the town. What could Howard Brighton have been thinking to do such a thing!"

They did not know how he had toiled and planned in his narrow little office down near the wharves of the seaport town, how he and his wife had dreamed together that their three children should live in some other place than on the cramped, stony street where they had been born. After his wife's death he had still gone forward with his dream and, when he found that he had, himself, not very long to live, he had made haste to build the cottage that they had so greatly desired.

"It is pleasure enough to think of the children's having it," he said to a plain-spoken neighbor who remonstrated with him on the ground that he could never live there. "The boys will be old enough to care for their sister, and the house on the hill will be just the place for a little maid to grow up."

His children were of widely separated ages, for Ralph, the eldest, was twenty-one, Felix seventeen, and Barbara, as has been said, only twelve. It happened also that they had not all of them the same tastes, for while the two younger ones loved the country and looked forward to living on the Windy Hill, Ralph's desire was to go on working in the dusty office where he had already begun to prosper.

"He is a good getter, but a poor spender," the neighbors said, and in this were right. Ralph, with his first success, had begun to think too much of money and too little of other things.

In the end the cottage was never finished, only the main portion, a tiny dwelling, was completed without the two broad wings with which Howard Brighton had meant to enlarge it and which he did not live to build. When their father had gone from them his children found that he had left everything he had to Ralph, since the laws of seventy-five years ago made some difficulty over property being held by those who were not of age.

"Ralph has a wise head on his young shoulders and will know how to take good care of the younger ones," was the comment of busy tongues.

Perhaps Ralph heard them, with the result that he felt older and wiser than he really was, but of that no one can be sure.

The Windy Hill

It was on a clear, warm day of mid-July when they moved from the airless street of the town to their new, wind-swept dwelling on the hill.

"It looks like home already," Barbara said as they came up to the door, for, with its wide, low roof, its broad windows, and its swinging half doors that let in the sunshine and the fresh breezes, it seemed indeed a place in which to forget their sadness and to find a new, happy life. The rustling voice of the oak tree above seemed to be bidding them welcome, and a tall clump of hollyhocks by the door-stone, shell pink and white, seemed to have come into bloom that very day just for their home-coming.

Barbara ran from room to room, exclaiming in delight over the new freedom, while the two brothers sat on the doorstep to look down over their new domain and to talk of the future. Their father had planned to turn the meadow below into an orchard, and had even managed to set out the first half of the little trees, slim, tiny saplings that dotted the sloping green.

"We will put in the others next autumn and spring," Felix said, "and I will be building new cupboards and shelves for old Chloe in the kitchen, I will mend the press in Barbara's room and I will finish off the garret chamber under the eaves for myself, and there I can play the fiddle to my heart's content and never disturb you at all. I think that life will be very pleasant here."

So their lives swung into the new channel, with Chloe, Barbara's old nurse, to cook for them and with Felix to tend the apple trees and the little garden, to saw and hammer and whistle all day at the task of setting the new place in order.

"It's a pity you haven't a proper, handsome house, with long windows from the ceiling to the floor and a high roof and a carved front door and with black marble chimneypieces instead of these rough stone fireplaces," Chloe would sigh, for she thought that the elegance of that time was none too good for the people she loved. It may be that Ralph sighed with her, but Felix and Barbara were frankly delighted with the painted floors, the casement windows, and the low, big-beamed rooms. In the evenings, as the two would sit on the wide doorstep, the voice of Felix's violin would mingle with the voice of the wind in the oak, while Barbara listened, entranced, for her brother was a real master of his instrument. It would laugh and sing and sigh, while Barbara pressed closer and closer to his knee while the stars came out and the evening breeze stirred the hollyhocks and the great branches of the oak tree. Ralph rode every day to the town to labor over heavy account books in his cramped little office and he always brought home a sheaf of papers under his arm. He would sit at the table inside the window in the candlelight and, as the music rose outside, singing to the child and the flowers and the stars, he would scowl and fidget and tap irritably on the table with the point of his pen, for he did not love his brother's playing.

"There is too much time spent on it," he would say, "when you might be doing useful things."

"I have no head for adding up your endless columns of dollars and cents," Felix would answer, "so I must make myself useful in my own way."

A warm, golden October had painted the valley with blazing colors, had turned the oak tree to ruddy bronze, and had afforded ideal weather for the further planting of the orchard. Here Felix was at work, with Barbara following at his heels, and helping, when each tree was planted, to hold it upright while he pressed down the earth about its roots.

"We will leave an open space through the center," he said, "a lane that will lead straight up toward the house, so that when Ralph and I come home we can look up to the open door and the hollyhocks around the step. Only," he shook his head regretfully, "I am afraid Ralph won't see the flowers. His head is too full of dollar signs when he comes home from the town."

The Windy Hill

Barbara turned about to look through the orchard. Some one came trudging along between the little trees, his heavy, tired feet crunching in the leaves.

"Oh, it's a peddler," she cried eagerly, for she was always pleased when these traveling merchants came past, with their laces and gay embroideries and colored beads to dazzle the eyes of little girls. But this was a peddler of another sort, a dark-faced man with melting black eyes and eager speech that was less than half of it English. He was an immigrant Italian, newly come to this great America, he managed to explain, and he was trying to sell the trinkets and small household treasures that he had brought with him.

They led him up to the house, for he was weary and hungry, and while Barbara brought him food, Felix was plying him with questions as to where he had come from and whither he was going. He had meant to settle down in the little seaport, so he told them, but—here he became so voluble that it was almost impossible to understand him—he did not wish to stop there now, he must go on—on.

"It is the gold," he cried excitedly, making wide gestures with both his brown hands, "the beautiful yellow gold. They find it everywhere!"

He brought out a tattered newspaper to let them see for themselves what he could not explain. News traveled slowly in those days, so that in this out-of-the-way corner of Medford Valley the brother and sister now heard for the first time of the discovery of gold in California. Yet in the towns and where people could gather to tell one another ever-growing stories, the world was rapidly going mad over tales of gold lying loose for the gathering, of nuggets as big as a fist, of rivers running yellow with the precious shining dust.

"Listen, Barbara; why, it can't be true!" cried Felix as he read aloud, the Italian interrupting excitedly, trying to tell them more. It was for this that he had abandoned his plans, that he was selling everything he had to follow a far, golden dream across the country to California.

"A terrible journey, they say," he admitted, "but what does one care, with such fortune at the other end?"

He had little left to sell, nor had they much money to buy; but, so carried away were they by his ardor, they would have given him anything they had. There was a carved ivory crucifix, a silver chain and, at the very bottom of his bag, a square box that gave forth a curious humming noise.

"Take care," he cautioned, as Barbara would have peeped within, "they fly away—the bees!"

"Bees?" she echoed in astonishment.

Yes, he had brought all the way to America a queen bee and her retinue of workers, for Italian bees, he told them gravely, were known the world over for their beauty, industry, and gentleness.

"They sting you only if you hurt them," he declared. "Other times, never."

He explained how they were to be put into a hive and just how they were to be tended, for he was wise in the bee lore of Italy. Felix had seen some of the farmers round about struggling with the wild black bees whose tempers were so vicious that the only way to gather their honey was to smoke the whole hiveful to death. The man opened the box a little way to let the yellow-banded creatures crawl over his fingers, to show their gentleness.

"I must sell them quick," he said, "for they live not much longer in a box."

They bought the bees, Felix and Barbara, though it took every penny they had in the house and even the store in the little carved box on the mantel which they were all saving, by Ralph's advice, against a rainy day. The man went away down through the orchard, turning to wave his ragged hat in joyful good-by, for now he had sold everything and was off and away to California.

The Windy Hill

Felix sat on the doorstep, watching him go, while Barbara moved about inside, laying the table for supper. A thought suddenly struck her and she went to the door.

"Felix," she said, "I wonder what Ralph will say?"

But Felix was not listening.

"Gold," he repeated softly. "Did you hear what he said, Barbara? The sands of the rivers yellow with it, the Indians giving their children nuggets to play with, a year's earnings to be picked up in a day!"

He was so lost in his dream that he could talk of nothing else. It was not the sort of gold that Ralph loved, minted coins that could be saved and counted and stacked away, but it was the shining treasure of romance, wealth that, unlike dully satisfying riches, meant battle and adventure and triumph after overwhelming odds. He did at last consent to help Barbara house the bees in a suitable dwelling, but he talked still of the tale he had heard and his eyes were shining with the wonder of it.

"Did you hear him say that there was just one beaten trail across the plains, all the way from the Mississippi to California? Think of a road, a single road, two thousand miles long, reaching out through the wilderness, over the deserts, through the mountains, with no towns or houses or people, just one lonely highway—and gold at the far end!"

Ralph was late that evening, late and tired and impatient after an unsatisfactory day. He brushed past Felix, still sitting on the step, flung down his bundle of papers, and went over to the fire. The little carved money box stood open on the mantel, revealing its emptiness.

"What is this?" he asked Barbara sternly, as she stood in the corner, twisting her apron and finding, suddenly, that it was very difficult to explain. Felix came in, the light of excitement still on his face, eager to tell the tale.

He began to recount what they had heard, so carried away that he never noticed the gathering thundercloud upon his brother's face. The

101

plains, the mountains, the shining rivers running to the sea—he seemed to conjure up all of them as he told the story, but Ralph's face never changed.

"So," cut in the elder brother at last when the younger stopped for breath, "it is for a fairy tale like this that you have wasted your time and your substance, have emptied my money box. You bought bees with it—bees! To buy bees when the forest is full of them and you can have a swarm from any neighbor for the asking. You spend my money that some lying rascal may be helped upon his way!"

"It was our money," Felix reminded him gently, beginning to be awakened from his dream by the bitter anger of the other's tone.

"Mine," repeated Ralph. A cold fury seemed to possess him, which discussions over money could alone bring forth. "Have you forgotten that everything here is mine, given me by our father? The bread you eat, the roof over your head, they belong to me; do you understand?"

Barbara saw, in the firelight, that Felix's face flushed, then turned white. No one but herself could know just how such words would hurt him, how his pride, his love for his brother, and his sturdy independence were all cut to the very quick. He went out of the room without a word and could be heard climbing the ladderlike stairs that led to the room he had made for himself under the eaves. Ralph sat down by the fire, muttering uneasily something about "it all blowing over." With lagging steps Barbara went on setting the table.

They were not prepared to see Felix come down the stairs a few minutes later with his coat and cap and with his violin under his arm.

"I will take no man's charity, not even my brother's," he said huskily, as he stood still for a moment on the threshold. Then he was gone.

Barbara leaned over the half door and watched him go down the path, saw him pass through the lane of tiny apple trees, saw the dusk gather about him as he went on, a smaller and smaller, plodding figure

The Windy Hill

that disappeared at last into the dark. The autumn wind in the oak tree sounded blustering and cold as she closed the door and turned back to the room again.

"He has only gone down to the town, he will come back to-morrow," growled Ralph, but Barbara knew better.

"He has gone to look for gold," she cried, and, sitting down on the bench by the fire, she buried her face in her hands and burst into tears.

Felix used to think, as the days and weeks passed, and as that strange journey upon which he had launched so suddenly dragged on and on, that the grassy slope above the orchard and the cool dark foliage of the oak tree must be the very greenest and fairest things on earth. There was no green now before his aching eyes, only the wide stretch of yellow-brown prairie, a rough trail, deep in dust, winding across it, a line of white-topped wagons crawling like ants over the vast plain, and a blue arch of sky above, blinding-bright with the heat.

It was October when he went away from home, it was a month later when, by leisurely stage and slow canal boat, he arrived at the Mississippi River, the outpost of established travel. Here he was obliged to wait until spring, for even in the rush of '49 there were few bold enough to attempt the overland trail in winter. He turned his hand to every sort of work, he did odd jobs during the day and played his violin for dancing at night, he grew lean and out-at-elbows and graver than he used to be. He slept in strange places and ate stranger food, he suffered pangs of hunger and of homesickness, but he never thought of going back. His violin went everywhere with him, and in more than one of the little towns along the big river, people began to demand the boy fiddler who could make such gay music for their merrymakings.

When at last the snow melted, the wild geese flew northward, and the wilderness trail was open again, he had no difficulty in finding an emigrant party to which to attach himself. Abner Blythe was a lean, hard Yankee, but he had lived for years in the Middle West and had made journeys out into the prairie, although he had never gone the whole of the way to the mountains and the coast. He knew how to drive cattle with the long black-snake whip, whose snapping lash alone can voice the master's orders and which can flick the ear or flank of a wandering steer at the outermost limit of reach. His frail, eager-eyed little wife was to go with them, their boy of five, and a company of helpers who were to drive the wagons of supplies and to serve for protection against Indians.

The road was crowded at first, and the prairie grass grew green and high, full of wild strawberries, pink wild roses, and meadow larks. But as they journeyed slowly westward, as spring passed into summer, the green turned to brown under the burning sun, the low bluffs and tree-bordered water-courses were left behind, and they came to the wide, hot plains that seemed to have no end. At the beginning they sometimes passed farmhouses to the right and left of the trail, built by some struggling pioneer, where there was a little stream of water and where a few trees were planted. The places looked to Felix like the Noah's Ark he used to play with when he was small—the tiny, toy trees, the square toy house, little toy animals set out on the bare, brown floor of the prairie. Even the gaunt women in shapeless garments who always came to the door to watch the wagon train go by were not unlike the stiff wooden figures of Mrs. Noah. At last, however, even the scattered houses came to an end and there was nothing before them but the wilderness.

It was desperately hot, with the blazing sun above and the scorching winds swooping over the prairie to blow in their faces like the blast of a furnace. They made long stops at noontime, resting in the shade of the

The Windy Hill

wagons and pressed on late into the night, so that not an hour might be lost. They went by herds of buffalo, big, clumsy, inert creatures, that looked so formidable from in front and so insignificant from behind. They saw slim, swift little antelope and, on the far horizon, they sometimes made out moving dots that must be Indians. Their numbers and their vigilance, however, seemed great enough to keep them safe from attack.

A deadly weariness began to fall upon them all, so that Abner Blythe became morose and silent, his wife looked haggard and hollow-eyed, the men grew irritable, and the animals lagged more and more. Others who had passed that way had left many of their footsore beasts behind them—horses, oxen, cows, and sheep—to fall a prey at once to the great gray prairie wolves that hung behind every wagon train, waiting for the stragglers who could not keep up.

"It is only the human beings who have the courage to go on," Abner Blythe said to Felix. "You would think that horses were stronger than men and oxen the strongest of all, but the beasts give up and lie down by the road to die, yet the men keep on. It is not strength but spirit that carries us all to our journey's end."

There was one high-spirited black mare, the dearly beloved of Felix's heart, who, whether dragging at the heavy wagon or cantering under the saddle, was always full of energy and fire. She was the boy's especial charge, and, as the weeks passed, the two became such friends as are only produced by long companionship and unbelievable hardships endured together. It was a dreadful hour when, one night as they were making camp, the little mare lay down and not even for a feed of oats or the precious lump of sugar offered her, would she get up again. The very spirit that had driven her forward more bravely than the rest had produced greater exhaustion now.

"We will have to go on without her," said Abner Blythe dejectedly, as they sat about the camp fire.

Felix was feeding the flame with the sparse fuel, and Anna Blythe, Abner's wife, was sitting on a roll of blankets with her child on her lap. The little boy was ill and lay wailing against her shoulder.

"Don't leave the mare," Felix begged. "A day or two of rest will cure her entirely. There is water here, and grass beside the stream. We could camp two or three days until she can go on."

Abner shook his head wearily.

"We have no time to waste," he declared. "It is August now and we must cross the mountains before the middle of September. We haven't a day, not even an hour, to lose."

Anna Blythe sighed a deep, quivering sigh. Felix knew that she loved the little horse, too, and, so he sometimes thought, she was herself so weary that she often longed to lie down beside the trail and perish as the tired dumb animals did. She had never made complaint before, but to-night, perhaps appalled by the thought of the mountains still to be crossed, she burst out into fierce questioning:

"Abner, why don't we turn back? What is it all for? Can gold, all the gold we could ever gather, repay us for this terrible journey? We are little more than halfway and the worst is still before us. We could go back while there is still time. Why do we go on?"

Abner, spreading his big hands upon his knees, sat staring into the fire.

"I don't know," he said at last, "I vow I don't know. It is not the excitement, nor the gold that drives us, there is no telling what it may be. Our country must go on, she must press forward to new opportunities, she must dwell in new places. It is through people like us that such growth comes about, we don't ourselves know why. A little ambition, a little hope, a great blind impulse, and we go forward. That is all."

They sat very still while the fire died out into charring embers and darkness filled the wide sky above them, showing the whole circling march of the stars like a sky at sea.

"We must be moving," Abner said at last, "we can make a few miles more before it is time to sleep."

They all arose wearily and made ready to go on. Felix went to where the black mare lay and passed his hand down her smooth neck. She whinnied and thrust her soft nose against his cheek, but would make no effort to move. He stood for a moment thinking deeply. Very clearly did he understand Abner's unreasoning desire to go forward, but, perhaps because he was only a boy, he did not feel that same wish so completely and passionately. There were other ideas in his mind, and uppermost among them was the feeling that one can not desert a well-loved friend. Just as the foremost wagon creaked into motion and rumbled forward into the dark, his resolution found its way into words.

"I think I will stay with the mare," he said. "In three days at least she will be rested enough to go on, and then I can easily overtake you. We don't want to lose her." He tried to hide the depth of his feeling with commonplace words. "It wouldn't be sensible, when we have so few horses."

Abner did not consent willingly, but he agreed at last.

"She'll travel fast when she is on her feet again," he said, "and I don't like leaving her myself."

Felix took some provisions from the cook's wagon, gathered up his blankets, slung his gun over his shoulder, and, as a last thought, reached in for his violin. It would be good company in the dark, he thought.

"Keep your gun cocked for Indians," were Abner's last instructions, "look out for rattlesnakes at the water holes, and catch us up when you can. Good luck to you."

The boy stood beside the trail and listened to the slow complaining of the wheels and the shuffling of the feet of horses and oxen in the dust as the whole train moved onward. For a little while he could hear them and could see the bulk of the wagon tops outlined against the stars, then the long roll of the prairie hid them and he was left all alone in the wide, wild, empty plain.

CHAPTER IX.

THE FIDDLER OF APPLE TREE LANE *(Continued)*

Felix tended the little horse as best he could, bringing her grass, which she would not eat and water, which she drank gratefully. At last, unbelievably tired, he built up the fire and lay down to sleep. His heavy eyes were just closing when he saw a black shadow move silently across the basin of the little watercourse and heard the crunch of a pebble dislodged by a softly padding foot. As he sat up, a big gray wolf, as unafraid as a dog, from long following at the heels of the emigrant trains, came out into the circle of light. With its head lowered and its eyes shining in the dark, it sat down—to wait.

The fire dwindled, for there was little to burn save the dried twigs from the bushes that lined the stream, nor did Felix dare to leave the horse long enough to gather a fresh supply. More gray figures came through the dark to gather in a wide, waiting circle all about the fire. Within the limits of their brutish minds lay the knowledge that fires would die down, that strength of man and beast would fail, and that, once a straggler could not go on, patient waiting always made him their prey at last. Felix cocked his gun, took long aim at a pair of green eyes glittering in the dark, but in the end lowered the muzzle without firing. The flash of a rifle and its report carried far over the level prairie, and there were other eyes that might be watching for human stragglers, fiercer and hungrier eyes even than were the wolves'. As the foremost animal drew a little closer, he took up his violin and began to play.

He had a strange audience, the greedy white-fanged beasts that slunk away at the first strains of the unwonted sound, stole back, yet moved uneasily away again, the little fat, inquisitive prairie dogs that popped out of their burrows and sat up to listen, the circling nighthawks that wheeled and called overhead. Hour after hour he played, but whenever he paused the hungry circle drew in about him and he was forced to raise his aching arm and ply his bow again. The first hint of dawn was brightening the sky when the creatures of the night began to slip away, and Felix, laying down his violin, suddenly laughed aloud.

"I wish that Granny Fullerton, who thought that it wasn't quite safe for us to live on the Windy Hill," he said, "I wish that she could see me now!"

Then he lay down, pillowed his head upon his arm, and fell so fast asleep that, as he said afterward, "a whole tribe of Indians could have ridden over him and he would never have moved."

It was, indeed, horse's feet that aroused him, but not, by good fortune, the unshod hoofs of Indian ponies. A band of men was riding toward him from the westward, hard, grizzled men, weather-beaten and toil-worn beyond anything Felix had ever seen.

"We met your party back yonder," said their leader. "They asked us to look out for you as we went by. Glad to see the Indians haven't got you yet."

"Oh!" exclaimed Felix, sitting up and rubbing his eyes, "Have you—have you been in California?"

The man nodded. He drew out of his pocket a greasy little buckskin bag, opened the strings, and poured a stream of something yellow into the boy's hand.

"Ever see gold dust before?" he asked.

The Windy Hill

It was Felix's first sight of the odd, flattened flakes of metal that shine dully in your hand, that are no two alike, so that you can turn them over and over, always seeing different shapes and sizes, different gleams and lights upon their changing surfaces.

"There's a lot of it back there where we've been," the man said, grinning slowly as he saw Felix's excited face. "We left it there for you and those like you."

"And did you find all you wanted? Are you going home now to be rich and comfortable all your days?" the boy inquired.

The man's grin grew broader still.

"You don't know gold miners, sonny," he said. "We've been at work on the American River diggings, where your folks ahead there are going, and we found it good enough, but we've heard of something better. Over to the southward of that valley there's another one deeper, wilder, hard to get into but with the richest pay dirt you ever dreamed of. We staked out our claims and left one man to hold it, while we go back to the States for supplies and better equipment. The gold's harder to get out, but it's there all right. It makes American River look like nothing at all."

He turned in the saddle and looked up the little stream bed where the water lay in shallow pools below the overhanging bushes. The black mare had at last struggled to her feet and was now grazing on the sparse grass that bordered the river.

"It is none too safe for you to be here alone, young fellow," the man observed. "There's a band of Indians have been doing considerable mischief around this neighborhood just lately. We've been hearing of them from every party as we came along."

"I'm not afraid," returned Felix stoutly. "One boy and one horse would be hard to find in this great wide prairie. Aren't you afraid you will meet the Indians yourselves?"

"Afraid!" The other laughed aloud. "Why, we're looking for them and it will be a sorry day for them when we find them." He sobered and went on earnestly: "The woman in that party you left called out a message for you as we came by. 'Tell him,' she said to us, 'that the horse is his and that he is to go back with you to the States. Tell him, God bless him,' she said. We'll be glad enough to have you if you care to come with us," he concluded.

Felix looked at the long, empty trail before him; he looked up at the prospector's hard brown face, and then at the little heap of gold dust in his hand.

"I'll not go back—just yet," he said. "There are things I must see first."

They rode jingling away, the sun glinting on their gun barrels and pistol butts until they disappeared in the shimmering hot distance of the dusty trail. Felix, as the heat of the day increased, led the mare up the watercourse to where the bushes were tall enough to afford a little shade. He, himself, crawled under a rock beside one of the pools and lay there very quietly, waiting for the long, sleepy day to pass. It was noontime, with the world so still that he could actually hear the water of the stream filtering through the sand as it ran sluggishly from pool to pool, when a new sound caught his attention. There was a shuffling of muffled feet, a stone dislodged from the bank above, the click of metal against metal, but every noise so stealthy and quiet that he could hardly believe he heard.

He did not dare to move, but peered through the branches of the bush beside him and saw a strange cavalcade passing on the high bank above, little brown and buckskin and piebald Indian ponies, their unshod hoofs stepping lightly and quietly over the dry grass, each with a painted, red-skinned rider, armed and decorated with all of an Indian's trappings of war. The feathered war bonnets that crowned their heads and reached to their heels were of every gay color, their fierce faces were daubed with red and ocher, they carried, some of them, guns, more of them rude lances

The Windy Hill

and bows and arrows. Felix was so near that he could make out the strings of beads and claws of wild animals about their necks, could see their red skins glisten, and could watch the muscles of their slim thighs move and ripple as they guided their wise little horses more by pressure of the knee than by use of the rude Indian bridles. Not one of them spoke, once a pony snorted in the dust, but that was the only sound as they moved past him and turned into the trail with their faces eastward. The whole procession might have been a vision—a mirage of the high, hot noontide and of the boy's tired brain. But after the men were gone and he had crawled out from his hiding place he could see the horses' footprints in the dust and could assure himself that they were real.

After a long time he heard shots, very faint and far away, lasting for an hour or more before the hush of the prairie fell again. The cool night came at last, and the little mare, visibly strengthened by the rest and grazing, came trotting to him, splashing happily through the water of the pool. Those gray enemies of the night before did not come near, nor, though he waited two days, watchful and alert, did any of the Indians return. He thought of that band of men he had talked with, hard, seasoned, and well armed for the struggle. From the very first he had felt little doubt as to what the issue of such a battle would be.

It seems too long to tell of how Felix mounted the mare at last and cantered away along the trail, rejoicing in swift motion again after the long wait and the crawling pace of the ox team. Nor can it be fully told how he and his friends toiled forward across the plain, over that dreaded stretch of desert that came at the far edge of it, up the tempest-swept, snow-covered mountains, until that wondrous minute when the endless bleak slopes suddenly fell away before them and they looked down into the wide green wonder of a new land. In less than a week from that day, Felix's long dream had come true; he was standing knee-deep in a rushing stream with a miner's pan in his excited hands, he saw the gravel wash away, the muddy earth dissolve, the black sand settle to the bottom to be dried and blown away, leaving—it did not even then seem believable—the sparkling grains of yellow gold.

They did well, he and Abner Blythe. Though their backs ached at the end of the day and they came home to sleep, worn out, wet, and dirty, their buckskin bags filled slowly with gold dust as the autumn passed. Yet Felix could not put from his mind the talk of the man he had met on the prairie, the tale of higher mountains, deeper valleys, and richer diggings over to the southward. When the rains came and there was little work to do, he thought of those words more and more, and when the open weather came once more he gathered supplies, said good-by one day to Abner and Anna, and set forth to seek a further, greater fortune for them all.

It was a toilsome journey over the mountains, for very few had as yet passed that way. The deep, shadowy cañons, the rushing streams, the smooth faces of granite walls seemed impassable barriers, but Felix at last passed them all and came into the wild, rugged valley of Bear Creek. He staked his claim, put up his little tent, and went down to the river to wash his first pan of gold. Yes, the prospector had been right; here in this bleak, far region the toil was much heavier, but the reward was unbelievably great.

There were not yet many miners who had come so far, but the one whose claim was next to Felix's and whose rough shanty stood almost side by side with his tent had been there among the first. He was a friend of those men from whom the boy had first heard of the place, and he willingly showed the newcomer the best slope for his claim and the easiest way to wash the gold.

"There's room for all, so far," he said. "The others below there on American River haven't had time to get discontented yet, but there will be a rush up here soon. When the place begins to be crowded there will be jumping of claims, and robbery and fights, with knives out and blood shed, just as you have seen it down there. But we will be peaceable and friendly here as long as we can."

The old miner seemed to take a great fancy to Felix and helped him with advice and kindness in unnumbered ways. He had built himself a little hut of pine logs roofed with bark as a better protection than a tent against the mountain storms. Felix sat there with him one night before the rude stone hearth, while the rain fell in deluges outside and the wind went calling and blustering down the valley. The miner piled the fuel high upon the fire and, as the hours passed, told story after story of wild adventure, of desperate escape, of bold crime, and of the quick, merciless justice of the frontier. At last his fund of narrative seemed to come to an end and he was silent for a little.

"Yes, these are rich diggings," he said finally, going back to the subject of which they had first been talking, "but—there is more gold even than this somewhere beyond. A man I knew once, a prospector, told me a strange story. He was captured by the Indians and carried off to the south, over beyond the mountains to the edge of the desert. He escaped from them, but he got lost, trying to go back, and wandered for days, nearly dying with thirst, torn and cut by the cactus thorns, blind and nearly crazed by the terrible heat. He came to the foot of a hill that he was too weak to climb and he lay down there to die. But a rain fell and he lay soaking in it all night, drinking what gathered in a rock pool beside him, with rattlesnakes and lizards, he said, crawling up to drink with him and he never cared. In the morning his head was clear and he looked up the hill to see the outcropping of such a gold mine as you never dreamed of. Lying there on the open slope was the gold-bearing quartz in plain sight, to be picked up with your bare hands. He took some with him, but not much, for gold is heavy when you are staggering weak, and he went on and on, lost again and nearly dead, but at last he came to a settlement. He lay in a Mexican's house, raving with fever for weeks, but in the end he got well. But when he tried to go back to his mine he could never find the way."

Felix was listening eagerly, but he did not interrupt or even ask a question when the man paused. The deep voice rasped huskily, for evidently the miner was telling his tale with an intent purpose.

"I have always meant, some day, to go and look for that mine myself, when I found a comrade I could trust, one who would not be afraid of the hardship and the danger. The way there is a terrible journey, but I believe I know almost to a certainty where the place must be. Will you come, boy—will you come?"

Felix got up and went to the tiny square window to look out. His voice was thick with excitement, but he did not answer directly.

"The storm has passed," he said, "and I must go back to my tent. I—I will think about what you say and tell you in the morning."

He went out into the dark, wet night, closing the door with a hand that shook and fumbled against the wooden latch.

The old miner must have slept little, for it was scarcely dawn before he had crossed the muddy slope to Felix's tent. Early as he was, the boy was before him, gathering up his possessions and thrusting them into his pack.

"You're going?" cried the man joyfully, but Felix shook his head.

"I'm going back," he said and beyond that he would tell him nothing.

He could not explain how, in the watches of the night, there had come to him the realization that the fever for finding gold is more consuming than the fever for getting it, that there is always the thirst to go on, to leave what one has and seek some new, dazzling discovery that seems just out of reach. To follow adventure is one thing; but, as the years pass,

The Windy Hill

to surrender a whole life to a single and selfish desire is quite another. Some indwelling wisdom had told Felix that it was time to turn back, but he had no words by which to make the other understand. The old miner had given up to the dream long ago; he would always be seeking something richer and better, always leaving it for some golden vision that would lure him forward until at last he would disappear in the mountains or the desert and never return.

"I am going to turn over my claim here to Abner Blythe," declared Felix. "It will make him rich and his wife happy, and you had better stay to work it with him, for I am going home."

"I can't stay." The miner seemed to understand also, but he was as brief and inarticulate as was the boy. "I'm one of those that has to go on—and on."

He turned away and walked back to his cabin through the rain-drenched flowers and the dripping green bushes. Who may know what pictures either of dark regret or of golden hope were passing before his eyes as vividly as were Felix's memories of the low cottage on the hill, of the apple trees that would be in bloom now all up and down Medford Valley, of the wind talking in the oak tree outside his window. A quarrel with one's only brother looks suddenly very small when so many thousand miles are stretched out between.

Ralph had often said that the hollyhocks were growing too many and should be uprooted, but Barbara's begging for their lives somehow always saved them in the end. They had spread out from the door and advanced down the hill in marching regiments, a glowing mass of color. The singing, yellow-banded bees were busy all day in the cups of scarlet fading to pink and white, and white shading into yellow. The afternoon sun was behind them, lighting them to unwonted glory, when Felix came plodding along the lane on each side of which the apple trees were beginning to grow tall. Barbara was in the garden cutting sweet peas into her apron and Ralph, beside her, was standing in silence, watching the bees. A dozen times the girl had read that same thought in his mind, that he would give ten years of life to unsay the words that had driven his brother away and that had taught himself such a bitter lesson. Then suddenly Barbara uttered such a cry of joy that even the bees hummed and hovered lower, and slow old Chloe came hurrying to the door. The old woman smiled, with tears running down her wrinkled face, as she saw who it was that came trudging up the hill.

"There's good luck come back to this house at last," she said aloud an hour later when Felix, as the twilight was falling, sat down upon the doorstep and began to play his violin.

He never grew tired of telling the tale of his adventurous journey, nor did his sister and brother ever grow tired of listening. Ralph Brighton had lost, in that one dreadful hour, his love for dollar signs, and he nodded in wise agreement over Felix's decision to give up the quest for gold. Barbara would hearken in awed fascination to that story of the man lost in the desert, whose eyes looked once upon fabulous wealth but who could never find it again.

Wherever gold mines are, there is to be found such a legend, a tale of greater riches just beyond men's knowledge. No matter how dazzling is the wealth at hand there is always that tantalizing story of the lost mine, sometimes reputed to be far and inaccessible, sometimes only just over the next hill, yet always as difficult to discover as the end of the rainbow. But, as Abner Blythe said, it is so a country grows, and when men cease from following rainbows, then will the world stand still.

CHAPTER X.

A MAN OF STRAW

The shower had lifted and was moving away down the valley, a gray mist of rain with a slowly following flood of sunshine. Oliver got up and said without enthusiasm:

"We must go now, we have an errand we must do. Come along, Janet."

She rose to go with him but looked back wistfully several times as she went, with lagging feet, down the hill. She had wished that the story might last forever, so that she need not face Anthony Crawford at the end of it.

They said nothing to each other as they climbed into the car and threaded the twisting lanes and byroads that would take them to the house they sought. Oliver was rehearsing within himself what he should say when they presented the picture. "My sister carried this away by mistake, we thought that we should return it to you as soon as possible.

"And then he will say something sharp and unkind, and I won't know what to answer," he reflected drearily. "I will want to say that I am sure it isn't his anyway and that Janet did well to take it, even by accident. But what is the use of stirring up more trouble? Well, I can only explain and then get away as quickly as we can."

It is probable that Janet, who sat by him in low-spirited silence, was really suffering less than he. Oliver had undertaken the responsibility of returning the picture, and Oliver was a dependable boy who could manage it far better than she could. She thought little of what was to be said or done and was only anxious to have the affair over.

They left the car in the lane and walked together toward the sagging gate. A man was just coming through it, who proved, as they came near, to be John Massey. His good-natured, friendly face was pale under its sunburn and drawn into unfamiliar lines of anger and despair.

"Mr. Peyton sent me the money to settle up my rent," he told them, "and I came up here to pay it and arrange about leaving. Crawford wants me to stay until the first of the month, but I am going to-day. He has never stocked the farm with the tools and machinery a landlord is supposed to furnish, so I've bought them myself, what I could, and now he says they are his. He wants to know how I can prove that I paid for them, when every one knows that it was his place to do it. He laughed at me when I said it would ruin me entirely. He said one man's gain was always from another man's loss. I vow there is the spirit of a devil in him."

He looked back at the house among the trees, clenching his big hands and muttering to himself in helpless fury.

"He just stood there grinning, even guessing my thoughts, for he said, 'You could knock me down, I know, but it would be no satisfaction to you, for I would get back at you through the law. It would cost you more than it is worth, John Massey.' It was what I knew was true myself, so I kept my hands off him and came away."

Janet and Oliver stood looking at him miserably, knowing that there was nothing to be done.

"Get into the car and wait for us," Oliver directed at last. "We will take you home when we have finished here. We won't stay long."

"You won't want to," observed John Massey bitterly. "He is in a famous bad temper."

They went through the gate with Janet's steps lagging more than ever. There was something almost uncanny about a man who could cause such misery to other people and yet go unscathed himself. They saw him almost

The Windy Hill

immediately as they came up the path. He had been cutting down some weeds in the neglected field and was standing in the middle of it, close beside the scarecrow. He did not move, but waited for them to come close, evidently meditating what he could say that would hurt and anger them the most. He began to speak the moment they came near, giving Oliver no opening for what he had meant to say:

"So Jasper Peyton, having sent one of you to steal my picture, has lost courage and sent two of you to bring it back again. Very clever, very clever of him indeed!"

"He knew nothing about it," Janet was beginning passionately, when Oliver silenced her by a touch on her shoulder.

"He knows that," he reminded her calmly; "he is only trying to make you angry."

He caught a look of smoldering fury in Anthony Crawford's eye and a note of surprised irritation in his voice.

"Well," the man snapped, "am I to have my property or not?"

"You are to have it. We will not keep anything that you even claim as yours," returned Oliver.

He felt hot rage surging up within him, yet he strove to keep it down. He had realized, of a sudden, that this man who could hurt his Cousin Jasper so deeply, who could ruin John Massey, could harm neither him nor Janet in the least. Oliver had felt real dread as he came through the gate, he had been haunted by the vague terror of what Anthony Crawford might be able to do, but he looked upon him now with disillusioned eyes, knowing him for nothing but a small-minded, selfish, spiteful man whose power over them was nothing at all.

"If I can only keep as calm as he can, he will never get the better of me," the boy thought desperately as he struggled with his own rising tide of anger.

"Perhaps you would be glad to have me establish my real rights," said Crawford. "You would like to have it brought up in court, perhaps, how your sister was found going through my possessions, and how she happened, quite by chance, of course, to select the most portable and valuable article in my house and carry it away with her. She would like, I am sure, to have public opportunity to make all that quite plain."

Oliver heard Janet's gasp of panic-stricken horror, but he still, by a great effort, retained his own presence of mind.

"We are not afraid of you," he asserted, looking straight into the other's narrow, shifting eyes. "I am nearly as big as you and I could roll you over and over in the mud of this wet field, only that would give you the legal hold on me that is just what you wish. You can't do us any real harm, no matter what you pretend. I don't believe you have anything behind those threats you make to Cousin Jasper, I don't think you believe in your claims yourself. You're a bluff; like this scarecrow here, you're nothing but a bogy man, stuffed with straw!"

He caught the scarecrow by the shoulder, venting his rage upon the helpless bundle of rags, shaking it even out of its ridiculous resemblance to its master, until it fell to bits about his feet. He flung down the miniature upon the heap of rags and, followed by Janet, walked away across the field. Anthony Crawford stood looking after him, never offering a word. When Oliver reached the path he became aware that John Massey was leaning over the gate, grinning in half-terrified delight. The rain was beginning to fall steadily again as they came out into the lane and climbed into the car.

It rained all of the afternoon, but ceased at nightfall, just in time, so Janet said, "to keep Mrs. Brown from nervous prostration." Oliver could not quite understand how plump, comfortable Mrs. Brown could be threatened with such a malady, for he had forgotten that next day there was to be a much heralded outing for all the members of Cousin Jasper's household. The occasion was a celebration at the next village, a glorified edition of the ordinary country fair in which farmers, summer visitors, and the residents of the bigger estates were all accustomed to take part. A magnificent affair it was to be with exhibitions, merry-go-rounds, peanut and lemonade stands, motor races, a horse show—something to please the taste of every variety of person. It was Cousin Jasper's custom to give the whole staff of servants a holiday for the festival, although the cook usually waited to serve an early lunch and Mrs. Brown came home before the others, to set out a late supper. No influence on earth could ever persuade Cousin Jasper to attend one of these merrymakings, but every other person under his roof was absorbed in looking forward to the great day of the summer. Elaborate preparations had been made and all that was now in question was the weather, for to make such an event a success it seemed absolutely necessary to have one of those clear, blazing-hot days that seem specially to belong to circuses, fairs, and midsummer festivals.

Janet was to go under the safe, but excited, wing of Mrs. Brown, and Oliver, also, was looking forward to the day with some anticipation.

"I wonder if the Beeman and Polly will be there," he thought, and went off into further speculation as to what the Beeman would look like in the more civilized clothes that such an occasion would demand. "I might not even know him," he reflected.

When the day came, however, cloudless, hot, just what such a day should be, Oliver suddenly announced that he was not going.

"I don't like to leave Cousin Jasper all alone when he is so worried," he said to Janet, but could not explain why there should be any cause for misgiving. "I didn't care a great deal about going anyway." He refused to listen to her suggestion that she should stay also.

Lines of motors were rolling down the road from early morning onward, filled with flannel-coated or befrilled holiday makers or laden with farmers and farmers' wives and farmers' children. Janet and Mrs. Brown, the one an excited flutter of white organdie skirts, the other a ponderous rustle of tight brown taffeta, departed at ten o'clock and by one the great house was empty of all save Oliver and Cousin Jasper.

The afternoon seemed very still and very long, as one hour followed another. Oliver strolled out to the gate and stood looking down the road, but the procession of motors had long since come to an end, so that the highway stretched, white and empty, to the far end of the valley. Yet as he stood, idly staring out in the hot quiet, he thought that he saw a small, dilapidated vehicle come round a distant turn and advance slowly toward him. When it was near enough for him to recognize the old white horse, the driver pulled up suddenly, turned the cart sharply about in the road, and rattled away in the direction from which he had come. Could it be that he had seen the boy there in the open gate, and therefore had decided not to come in? Oliver could scarcely believe that this was the reason.

An hour later, when he had gone back to the house, he saw a ragged, barefoot youth in faded overalls come shuffling up the drive. He delivered to Oliver a letter addressed to Cousin Jasper and said it was "from Mr. Crawford and he was to be sure to get an answer."

Oliver carried it away to the study and stood waiting, looking out through the window, while Cousin Jasper should read it and write a reply. The brightness of the holiday weather seemed to be growing dim somehow; the sun was still shining but with a touch of greenish, unreal light.

"I hope there isn't going to be a storm," he thought. His reflections were interrupted by a sound in the room behind him; Cousin Jasper was tearing the letter sharply to pieces.

"Anthony has sent what he calls an ultimatum," he said, trying to smile and not succeeding. "Tell the boy there is no answer."

The messenger, on being so informed, seemed reluctant to believe it.

The Windy Hill

"He said I must have one, not to come back without it," he kept insisting.

How Anthony Crawford had found any one to carry his letter on this day when Medford Valley seemed quite emptied of inhabitants seemed rather a mystery, yet he had not only found one but had impressed him forcibly with the necessity of fulfilling his errand. It was only after he had received a coin from Oliver's pocket and a large apple from the fruit dish in the dining room, that the shabby youth finally decided to go away.

"He said I wasn't to come back without an answer, so if I haven't one I needn't go back at all." He seemed to find this solution of the difficulty an excellent one and went striding away, whistling cheerfully.

Whatever final threat Anthony Crawford's letter had contained, it seemed to be unusually disturbing to Cousin Jasper. Having evidently made up his mind to ignore it, he seemed, just as plainly, to be able to think of nothing else. He seemed unwilling to be alone, and yet to be very bad company, for he was restless, silent, and, when Oliver, with an effort, tried to talk of cheerful things, was completely inattentive. They went into the garden at last to see how the flowers were faring. The sunshine was more unreal than ever, and sudden, fitful gusts of wind were beginning to stir the trees. They had inspected the flowers and were halfway across the lawn on their way to the house when the sun vanished, the wind rose to a roar, and, before they could reach the steps, the blinding rain was upon them.

It was not an ordinary thunderstorm, but one of those sinister tempests that occasionally break the tension of a hot summer day. Oliver, inside the hastily closed windows, could see the trees lashing helplessly, and could hear them groaning and snapping as one great branch after another came crashing to the ground. It was only a few minutes that the furious wind lasted, as it swept across the garden, but it left destruction in its wake. The beds of lilies were drenched and flattened, the smooth lawn was strewn with twigs and broken boughs, half a dozen trees were split, and one huge Lombardy poplar, with a mass of earth and roots turned upward, lay prone across the driveway.

It was half past six by Oliver's watch, then seven, then eight. No one had come home. Cousin Jasper was growing more and more restless and overwrought, Oliver was anxious—and hungry. He saw his cousin gather up the fragments of the letter, piece them together for rereading, then fling them from him once more. The boy wandered about aimlessly in the solitude of the big house, wishing that this long miserable day would reach an end and that Janet and Mrs. Brown would come home. It grew dark and no one returned, although, after a long time, the telephone began to ring.

It was Mrs. Brown's voice, nervous and only half audible, that sounded at the far end. Yes, she and Miss Janet were quite safe, they had been under shelter during the storm, but there had been such damage by the wind that both the railway and the road were blocked. They would not be able to get home for some hours, she feared.

"Could you, Mr. Oliver, just slip down to the kitchen and make poor Mr. Peyton a cup of tea and some toast? It is so bad for him to wait so late for his dinner. You will find the tea in the right-hand cupboard and the butter——"

The unsatisfactory connection cut her off, leaving Oliver standing aghast at her suggestion. "Just slip down to the kitchen," indeed, when he did not even know the way to that region of the house. And make tea! It seemed an utterly impossible task.

Through the long vista of rooms he could see Cousin Jasper in his study, sitting before his desk, and, fancying himself unseen, suddenly bowing his head in his hands.

"It won't do," thought Oliver determinedly, "he must have some one to help him, some one that knows more about this wretched business.

The Windy Hill

There is that Cousin Tom he talks about, Eleanor's father. I can't think of any one else. I will send for him."

If he could only have found the Beeman! He even searched the telephone book for the name of Marshall, but found none. And he had never discovered where the Beeman and Polly lived. Yes, the only choice was Cousin Tom.

He got the connection with some difficulty and asked for Mr. Brighton.

"Mr. Brighton is at dinner," returned the smooth voice of a well-trained servant; "he cannot be interrupted."

"But this is very important," insisted Oliver. "I am quite sure that if he knew——"

"My orders are that he is not to be disturbed," was the politely firm answer while the boy raged and fumed impotently.

"Then tell him," Oliver directed, "that his cousin, Mr. Jasper Peyton, is in very great trouble and needs to see him as—as soon as he finds it quite convenient."

His voice was trembling with anger and he slammed down the receiver without waiting for a reply.

"There was no use sending for him, after all," he reflected in black discouragement. He was not used to such treatment nor did he think that a man should surround himself with so much ceremony that he could not hear a plea for help. "He is just what Cousin Eleanor's father would be," was his disgusted verdict. "I was a fool to hope for any help there. If it had been the Beeman——"

Never had the house seemed so enormous or so silent as it was to-night. He went out through a swinging door, attempting to find the kitchen, fumbling down a passage, feeling in likely places for electric buttons, and not discovering them. He bumped his head against unexpected doors and cupboards, he upset something with a horrifying crash in the butler's pantry. At last he found the right door and the proper light switch, and stood in the big, shining white kitchen, looking about him helplessly at all the complicated apparatus of cookery, clean, polished, and complete, and utterly useless to him.

"This is no place for a boy," he exclaimed stormily after he had pinched his fingers in a drawer, spilled the water, and produced a roaring, spitting flame in the gas burner that blew up in his face and then went out. After fifteen minutes of miserable effort he at last heard the water boil noisily in the kettle where he had placed water and tea together. He poured out a cupful of the poisonous brew and stood regarding it in despair.

"I wish Mrs. Brown would come home," he groaned. "I'd be glad of any woman, any girl, even Cousin Eleanor."

He had opened a window, for the place was hot and close and through this he could hear, of a sudden, the sound of an automobile coming up the drive. He dashed through the dark passage, hurried to the great front door, and flung it open. There was a crunching of big wheels on the gravel and the snorting of an engine checked suddenly to a stop. It was not Mrs. Brown and Janet, for, though he heard voices, they were not theirs. The car had stopped beyond the fallen tree and some one was coming across the grass—two people, for the voices were a man's and a girl's. Apparently Cousin Tom had not stopped to finish his dinner, after all, and he had brought Cousin Eleanor.

"Yes, I'll be glad to see even her," he thought desperately.

The two came nearer, a man in white flannels, but bareheaded in the hurry of his coming, and a girl in white also. There was something familiar in the swing of those broad shoulders, in the tone of that voice. Yet Oliver stood, blinking stupidly, holding to the side of the door, too dazed to speak when the two stepped out of the dark and came up the steps—the Beeman and Polly.

CHAPTER XI.

THREE COUSINS

"Good gracious, Oliver, do you mean to say you really did not know? We used to talk it over, Polly and I, and wonder whether you were not beginning to see through us. Janet had some suspicions, and when she met us at the fair this afternoon, she understood who we were at last. Now I will present you to Miss Eleanor Marshall Brighton, known to her own family as Polly. I would not have broken this thing to you so suddenly, if I had taken time to think."

Oliver listened to Cousin Tom's half-apologetic explanations, yet he scarcely heard them, but still stood leaning against the doorpost, gaping with astonishment. Of course he had always known that there was something unusual about the Beeman, but as to who he really was he had never had an inkling. And this was Cousin Eleanor, the girl he had pictured so definitely that it seemed she could not be other than the prim, detested person he had so dreaded meeting. It was the very vividness of his idea of her that had stood in the way of his guessing the truth. But if the Beeman were really Cousin Tom, then he could, of course, put everything right and—more immediate cause for rejoicing—Polly could cook!

"Oh, come down to the kitchen and get Cousin Jasper something to eat," he begged. "He is almost starved. It is half past eight and he had lunch at twelve."

He gave Tom Brighton a rapid account of what had happened that day—of the letter, of Cousin Jasper's increasing agitation, of his final desperate call for help on his own responsibility.

"Poor Oliver, what a day you have had, while the rest of us were enjoying ourselves at the fair!" said Cousin Tom. "Polly and I happened to come home early before the storm, so that your message found us and we came at once."

"And he is starved himself," put in Polly. "He has not had anything to eat any more than Cousin Jasper."

It was wonderful to watch Polly making short shrift of the remains of his own awkward preparations, to see her skillful manipulation of the gas burners and her marvelous dexterity with the egg beater. And this slim, eager, shy Polly, with her crinkled brown hair and her freckled nose, this was really Eleanor Brighton. Oliver sat down limply upon one of the kitchen chairs to contemplate the wonder of it anew.

"I did not know who you were, myself, that first day," she said, "though Daddy guessed at once and even suspected that you were planning to go away. Janet told us all about it this afternoon, how Cousin Jasper made such a mistake and thought that he could force you to meet a girl that you were sure you wouldn't like. I would have done just the same myself if my father had tried to make me meet you, only he is too wise for such a thing."

But Oliver could only shake his head and marvel that he had not guessed.

Later, after Cousin Jasper and Oliver had feasted on the supper of Polly's providing, they all gathered about the table in the library and Cousin Tom unlocked the battered old strong box that he had brought in from the car.

"As I am the family lawyer," he explained to Oliver—"yes, bees are only a hobby, and my real business is the law—I have in my possession

The Windy Hill

most of the records belonging to this affair. I have gone into the whole matter of Anthony's claims from the very beginning and I am prepared to fight him for every inch that he demands."

He began taking papers from the box, fat rolls of legal documents, letters with their edges worn into tatters and addressed in the crabbed writing of a century ago, title deeds discolored and yellow with age, most of them fastened with great red seals, a mass of musty records that looked dry and dull indeed.

While he was spreading them out upon the table, the door opened quietly and Janet slipped in. She assured them that she had dined and had not got wet, that, except for Mrs. Brown's terrible fever of anxiety lest Cousin Jasper should not be properly cared for, all had gone well. Might she listen, please, and was there going to be another story?

"Not of just the same kind that I have been telling you up yonder on the Windy Hill," replied Tom Brighton, "although here you see the source of all those tales and of a hundred others like them. They are all buried here in these dusty papers, the history of your forbears and of the lands in Medford Valley. It goes all the way back, does the record, to the time when our several times great-grandfather bought the first tract from the Indian, Nashola. I am always glad to think that the red man had enough intelligence and the white man enough honor to make something like a real bargain, that this valley was purchased for what the wild lands were worth instead of being paid for with a gun, a drink of bad spirits, and a handful of beads. See, here is Nashola's name; he learned to write after a fashion, although the Indian witnesses signed only with a mark. And here is the signature of that first one of our kin to settle in the New World, Matthew Hallowell."

"Hallowell?" echoed Oliver. "Did he belong to those same Hallowells in the story, who quarreled over the Huntress?"

131

"Yes," was the answer, "he was the beginning of a vigorous line, living in and near Medford Valley until there came at last the Hallowell who moved to the seaport town, who built his first ship there and launched into foreign trade. They became great merchants, the Hallowells, in that time between the Revolution and the War of 1812 when Yankee ships and Yankee owners were lords of the high seas. But fortune failed after the death of Reuben Hallowell; his son Alan loved sailing rather than trading and his daughter Cicely married a junior partner in a lesser firm, Howard Brighton, who thought it better for his sons and daughter to go to live on the lands in Medford Valley that had belonged to their mother and had been given by her to him. Cicely's children were Ralph and Felix and Barbara Brighton, of all of whom you have heard."

"How have they heard, Tom?" asked Cousin Jasper, and the Beeman smiled.

"I have been filling up their minds with family history, for I knew that they must understand about this whole affair some day and it would take too long to tell them all the facts at once. So we have come now to the latest portion of the story," he went on, turning again to the younger members of his audience, "to a period when three cousins, Jasper Peyton, Anthony Crawford, and Tom Brighton used to spend much time together when they were growing up.

"Jasper and I are first cousins, since my father was Ralph Brighton and his mother was that younger sister, Barbara. I have had no reluctance in telling you of that bitter mistake my father made and the quarrel with his brother, for he spoke of it often himself and said that, in all his life, he never learned a more valuable lesson. Felix did not marry, since his zeal for the orchard and the bees and later for farming on a larger and larger scale seemed to occupy his every thought. It was he who reclaimed the marshy, waste ground in the valley, 'for,' he said, 'it is wrong that we on the seaboard leave our home acres and move farther and farther westward, looking for new land that is easy to till. It is a wasteful policy, even for a new country.' That was one of the things he had learned on his long journey across the West and back again."

"But I do not understand about Anthony Crawford," put in Oliver. "I haven't seen yet where he comes in at all."

"He calls us cousin, but it is a distant kinship, since he is grandson of that Martin Hallowell who broke with his partner Reuben over the matter of the Huntress. He used to come often to stay in Medford Valley, for he had been left without parents and Felix Brighton was his guardian. My Aunt Barbara, Jasper's mother, had lost her husband early, and she went to live with her brother Felix in the yellow stone farmhouse that had come to him from some earlier Hallowell who had built it a hundred years ago. How we loved the place and how happy we all were there, for I spent almost as much time under that wide, friendly roof as did Anthony. How patient and good Jasper's mother was to three mischievous, active boys, and how unceasingly, wisely kind was Felix Brighton! He has done much for us, Jasper and me, and he would, if he could, have made a man of Anthony.

"He was not like the other two of us, we could see that even when we were children. He was quicker and more clever than we, and he was better, or at least wiser, at holding his tongue and keeping his temper when the occasion served. But the key to his whole character was that he could never see any possession in the hands of another without instinctively wishing to have it for himself. I have seen him move heaven and earth to get something that he did not really want, merely because it seemed of value when it belonged to some one else. There was no one more clever than he at acquiring what he desired.

"Felix Brighton prospered greatly, but he never moved out of the comfortable farmhouse of which we were all so fond. It became very beautiful under his hands, extended and improved and filled with the rarest treasures of his gathering. He was especially fond of pictures, so that there was a wealth of portraits and landscapes that he had collected or inherited, that glowed like jewels on the mellow old walls. He did us unnumbered kindnesses when we were boys, and when, on growing up, we decided that we would all three be lawyers, he set us up as partners, Peyton, Crawford & Brighton. We felt very important with our law books, our profound knowledge, our newly painted sign and very little else. Even while we were studying, it was plain that Anthony, in his erratic, changeable way, was the cleverest of us all.

"And then history repeated itself, as it so often does. The grandson of Martin Hallowell and the two great-grandsons of Reuben fell out with each other over just such a questionable enterprise as had wrecked a partnership a hundred years ago. I can see him now as he came hurrying into our office that day full of the plan for his great scheme—just a quibble of the law and the thing was done. We were all to be made rich and successful by it, he explained. There is no use in describing to you the intricacies of his idea; it was one of those shoal waters in which the honesty of young lawyers can sometimes come to grief. The pursuit of law will winnow out the true from the false; it makes an upright man a hundred times more certain and more proud of his honor: it searches out the small, weak places of a meaner man's soul.

"Anthony tried to make this project sound quite simple and straightforward, but I can remember how narrowly he watched us and how, when he attempted to laugh at our objections, his voice cracked into shrill falsetto, under pressure of his excitement. I would have argued with him, explained, tried to dissuade him, but Jasper scorned my temporizing and would have had none of it. His sense of justice blazed high within him and his words leaped forth, a very avalanche of scorn and wrath.

The Windy Hill

Anthony heard him through without replying, then turned on his heel and went out. Our partnership was at an end. Later we heard that he had become involved with his scheme even before he spoke to us, that he had made himself liable for a sum of money, and that, to pay it—don't wince, Jasper, these children must know the truth—to pay it he forged Felix Brighton's name.

"There is something very terrible in the sudden destruction of your confidence in some one you have loved and trusted. Anthony is greatly changed now, although there is still a little of his old charm left. Yet you would not think of him as some one who had been an intimate part of our lives, a comrade whose cleverness we admired and whose honesty we had never doubted. And then he was suddenly blotted out of our existence. The wrong he had done was hushed up, he disappeared somewhere in the West, and it seemed that we were never to hear of him again. The years went by, Jasper's mother and then our Uncle Felix went from us. He had given me the lands on the west side of the river, since I was already owner of the cottage, the Windy Hill, and the bees that he had taught me to tend and love. To Jasper he had given the yellow stone house that had been like home for us all and his intimate possessions, the treasures it contained. He had given him also the drained farm lands by the river, a legacy that was an occupation in itself. He had seen that Jasper's bent was not really for the law, but that his best calling was the care of such an estate as this. More years passed, I became more and more absorbed in my own work down in the seaport town that has become a city, spending my holidays and my vacations in caring for the bees, not seeing Jasper so often, for he was over-busy also. And then Anthony came home.

"Whatever he had been doing in all this time we have no way of knowing. He had altered greatly, so that there seemed nothing left of his old self except his cleverness, some lingering affection for the place where he had been happy as a boy, and that old habit of coveting what other people had. He came back with a claim to make, one that went back as far as the day when Reuben and Martin Hallowell quarreled and made a hasty division of what had belonged to them in common. There had always been a slight doubt as to the title of the land upon which the yellow stone farmhouse stood, and to the upper end of the farms by the river. Anthony knew of it from the days when we studied law together and he came back determined to make that property his. I will not deny that he had some slight basis for his claim. He would accept no compromise or offer of purchase, so in the end Jasper gave in to him."

Cousin Jasper had not spoken throughout Tom Brighton's recounting of the whole affair. But now he took up the tale himself, going over the ground that, very evidently, he had pondered and argued and weighed within himself a hundred times.

"I had much and he had nothing, he was in real want and had a wife and two children besides. There was, as Tom says, some real basis for his claim since the title had never been made quite clear. And there is, further, no more bitter thing than a family quarrel, a division over the settlement of property, this one asking for what is more than his, that one fighting to hold what is not his own—no, it was unthinkable. So we settled the matter peaceably enough. I built a new house above him on the hill and he settled down in the place that had been home to all of us. He seemed to have repented of the wrong he had done and we were ready to forget it. I do not think that I ever doubted the honesty of his purpose, at first. Then it came to my wishing for some of the old possessions for my new house and he vowed that every one of them was his."

"I know," said Janet, nodding quickly. "He wouldn't give up the pictures, though he did not care for them himself. They were stored in the dust and dirt under the eaves and he asked me if you had sent me to see where he kept them. He only wanted them because they were yours."

"I suppose he meant to sell them some day," Cousin Jasper answered, "for there were several that were of almost as much value as the house itself. But less than ever was I willing to bicker and haggle over what I had really loved, and since he would not sell them to me I gave the matter up. Even then, there was a little justice on his side, for the pictures had been purchased with money from the lands that he called his. But it was my great mistake, since he did not understand at all why I yielded to him, and from that time he made certain that he had but to force me and I would relinquish everything."

Oliver muttered something angrily and went to stand by the window. He wanted a minute to think it out, to understand clearly before the tale went on. He could see just how Anthony had read Cousin Jasper's character, sensitive, high-strung, with strong affections that not even great wrongs could quite break down. But how mistaken the man had been who thought Jasper Peyton was a weak-willed person to be led anywhere!

"His success in getting made him greedy for more," went on Cousin Jasper, "and he began to push his claims further and further until I verily believe he began to think that everything I had should be his own. When I refused to yield one more inch, then the difficulties began indeed. He let the old house fall into unbelievable disrepair and he took the stand that since I was defrauding him, he was too poor to do otherwise. I built the high wall across the garden so that I need not see the home I had loved dropping to pieces before my eyes. At that his anger seemed to pass beyond control. He claims this, and he claims that, but I know that his final aim is the whole of what I have. He sent me a letter to-day, I do not understand why he did not come himself. He says that he is about to take public action, that he will bring into court the story of how Felix

Brighton became his guardian and used that position as a blind to live in possession of Anthony's inheritance. Oh, I cannot repeat it all, his threats against our good name and against the memory of those who are gone."

Cousin Jasper's voice dropped wearily into silence. Oliver dug his hands deep into his pockets and stood staring and scowling out through the window although all that he saw was the blackness outside and the dim reflection of his own face upon the pane.

"Our Uncle Felix never had the least notion that Anthony had a claim upon the place," Tom Brighton was saying behind him. "It was a legal technicality that Anthony was clever enough to find and make the most of. I do not at all believe in his right to it, even yet."

"He doesn't believe in it himself," Oliver made his declaration, whirling suddenly about upon them. "I told him that he was only bluffing and he could not even deny it. How I hate him," he cried huskily. "It is lucky that there are none of your bees near by, just now!"

Jasper Peyton looked at him in blank inquiry, but the Beeman smiled, yet shook his head at the same time.

"It is not only bees that are destroyed by hating," he said, "it is every good thing in life that dries up and blows away under the force of dislike and bitterness. Look at Anthony, who vows he has no affection for any one, who does not believe in friends or kindliness. He has hurt others, he has brought no happiness to himself, and, unless I am mistaken, he is going to wreck his whole scheme in one tremendous crash that we cannot now foresee. A lawyer, like myself, sees many hard, miserable, sordid things, but a Beeman has leisure to speculate as to whither they tend. And they all tend to the same thing."

They sat for some time about the table, explaining, discussing, and questioning, until finally the muffled booming of the clock in the hall proclaimed the hour of ten. Polly's eyes were beginning to look heavy, a fact that did not escape her father's watchful observation.

"These girls have had a long day and it is time for them to be in bed," he announced. "We have been over this whole matter and made things clear, and we have only to decide, since we are to fight Anthony in court, just what stand we will make. We will talk that over, Jasper, while Oliver takes your car and drives Polly home."

"I'll go with them," said Janet, jumping up also. She had been listening, bright-eyed and alert, through all of the story and showed no signs of sleepiness. Oliver tore himself away with some regret, for he did not wish to miss a word of the plans the two men were making. But Polly was evidently weary and ready to go home.

"Come along, Cousin Eleanor," he said briskly, and the three went, laughing, out through the door and down the steps.

It was very dark when Oliver brought out the big car and, skirting the fallen tree, made his way carefully down the drive. A bank of clouds to the eastward was all that was left of the storm, however, and through this the moon was breaking, with promise to rise clear, and come out into an empty sky. Oliver slowed down the car as they came to the gate and stopped for a moment to consider. The wind had dropped so completely that they could hear every sound of the summer night, even the dull, far-off roar of the flooded river.

"Do you know," he began slowly, "we never remembered to tell them that John Massey has left his place. I don't think any one but ourselves knows that he went away immediately; they will be thinking that he is still there, watching the dike. And to-night—listen how loud the river sounds!"

"Suppose we go down and look," said Polly. "It will not take us long and the road runs close to the bank."

He turned the car accordingly and they sped down the steep road, the sky growing brighter above them and the darkness fading as the moon came out. When they reached the last incline the whole of the valley lands, spread below them, were so flooded with light that the broad picture looked like an etching—white fields, black trees with blacker splashes of shade, sharp-cut, pointed shadows of houses and farm buildings, the silver expanse of the river, and the straight, white ribbon of the road. It was all very still and peaceful, with scarcely a light in any house and no single moving figure upon the highway. Medford Valley, worn out with its day of merrymaking, was wrapped in heavy sleep. Very strangely, the sight of this unsuspecting, slumbering community seemed to fill them all with sudden misgiving.

"I hope there's nothing wrong," muttered Oliver, swinging the car into its highest speed as they dashed down the road.

John Massey's house lay still and dark in the moonlight, its windows staring with the blank eyes that an uninhabited dwelling always shows the moment home life has gone out of it. They stopped the car near his gate and climbed out, all three of them, to walk at the foot of the high, grass-covered bank and search for signs of danger. It looked firm and solid enough, with its thick, green sod, its fringe of willows along the top, but with the whispering haste of the river sounding plainly against its outer wall. Standing on tiptoe, they could catch sight of the swift, sliding water, risen so high that it touched the very top of the bank. The roar of the swollen current could be heard all across the valley, but it was not so ominous, somehow, as the smaller voices of the ripples sucking and gurgling so close to their ears.

They walked along, three ghostly figures in the moonlight, until Janet, who happened to be ahead, stopped suddenly.

"I hear something strange; I don't understand what it is," she said.

Oliver stepped forward, bending his head to listen. Yes, he could hear it, too.

The Windy Hill

The sound was a soft hissing, as though a tiny snake might be hidden in the grass at their feet. But there was no grass thick enough for such shelter, only a few sparse stalks, rising in a drift of sand at the foot of the dike. The noise was made by the moving of the sand particles, as they stirred and seethed, with drops of water bubbling between them like the trickle of a spring. As they watched, the round wet space widened; it had been as big as a cup, now it was like a dinner plate.

"It's a leak in the bank." Oliver regarded it intently, thinking it quite too small to be dangerous. "I ought to be able to put my thumb in it," he added cheerfully, "but either there is something wrong with that Dutch story or there is something wrong with this hole."

"It isn't a joke," said Polly quickly. "They always begin that way. It—oh, run, run!"

For the boiling circle of sand had changed suddenly to a spout of muddy water that shot upward, spreading into a wide, brown pool that came washing over the grass to hide the spot where they had stood a moment before. From the higher ground of the road they watched it follow them, rising, pausing a little, then rising again.

"Back up the car or you will have to drive through the water," directed Polly. "Henry Brook's is the nearest house where we can find help. If that leak is to be blocked, the men will have to be quick."

They were in the car, Oliver had backed it round almost within its own length, and they were flying up the road before Polly had finished speaking. "Once, years ago, this long stretch of dike caved in and the whole current of the river came roaring down through the bottom lands. But there were no houses here then."

They came to a crossroad, turned into it, and stopped short before a gate. Oliver did not take time to open it, but tumbled over the top, raced across the grass, and thundered at the door of a dark, silent house. Oh, why did country people sleep so soundly? He knocked and knocked again and, after what seemed an interminable time, saw a light above and heard a window open.

"What do you want?" The farmer's big voice sounded none too pleased, but it changed quickly when Oliver told his news. "A break in the dike? Where? On Anthony Crawford's land, is it? Well, that's just where it would be. We don't any of us, around here, have much friendship for Crawford. Of course if the leak is very bad it will threaten us all. I'll spread the alarm while you go to get Mr. Peyton."

They were away up the road again; but, fast as they flew, the news seemed to travel faster. The rural telephone and the comfortable country habit of "listening in" on every message can spread tidings broadcast at a moment's notice. The largest farm, at the foot of the valley, had a great bell swung above its central barn, a bell whose excited voice could carry but one of two messages—flood or fire. Before they were halfway up the hill its wild clanging was calling all across the valley.

Up Cousin Jasper's avenue they came with a rush, flung themselves out of the car, and ran to the house. The two men were still bending over the papers, Cousin Jasper, with his thin, intent face, listening, Tom Brighton talking steadily, his eyes alight with that cheerful, eager kindliness that had so drawn Oliver to him from the first moment. They both turned in astonishment as the three came bursting in.

"A break in the dike at John Massey's place? And where was John Massey?" Cousin Tom questioned sharply. "Gone? If we had known that he had left, neither Jasper nor I would have been sitting here so quietly all evening, with the river in flood. And you have given the alarm? That is good."

There was a bustle of hasty preparations, but they were still standing in the hall when there came the sound of flying wheels on the drive and the uneven hoofbeats of an uncertain old horse urged to utmost speed.

"It's Anthony Crawford," said Oliver suddenly.

The man came in, the outcast cousin who had turned his hand against them all. His face was white, his gray eyes were burning with excitement, his voice was harsh and choked when he tried to speak.

"The dike—I see you know already. I went down over the hill to look and saw the moonlight on that pool of water. It was at John Massey's place. I came to get help."

Cousin Tom alone answered.

"Why was John Massey gone?" he said.

Oliver stepped forward to Tom Brighton's side and looked curiously at the man who been their enemy. He could see his hands shake as they crushed his battered old hat between them.

"We had quarreled," Anthony Crawford explained, his voice suddenly gone little and husky. "I turned him away three days ago and—and we had some words, so that he wouldn't stay even overnight after that. He watched the dike—and now the water is coming in."

One more question Cousin Tom asked.

"Why did you come to us?" he inquired steadily. "It would have been quicker to go down through the fields to the farms in the valley, to call out Henry Brook and send him with men and shovels and sandbags to stop the flood. To get here is a mile by the road and there was no time to lose." He pressed his question mercilessly. "Why did you come to us?"

Anthony Crawford moistened his dry lips, but he did not speak. There was a pause, though all of them knew that every second the waters of Medford River were sweeping higher and higher. It was finally Tom Brighton who answered his own question.

"You were afraid to go elsewhere. It was your doing, this flood; you took the land, you neglected the dikes, you sent John Massey away who would have watched against such a disaster as this. You were afraid to face those men, below, and tell them what you had done."

The other nodded.

"I haven't a friend in Medford Valley to help me—except you. Yes, I was afraid to face them; the break is in just the place where it may flood the whole bottom land. I thought they wouldn't move to help me until it was too late. And, on my life, Tom Brighton, if we can stop the flood I do not care what becomes of me."

It was quite true, as they could all see, that the man's desperate terror was not all for himself, that the situation was far too bad for that. He was picturing how the whole torrent of Medford River might soon be sweeping across those fields of ripening grain, those comfortable barns with their cows and sheep and horses, those pleasant white farmhouses where a hundred people lay asleep. He was seeing how, little by little, he had built up the wrong that was to be his ruin, he had driven away his friends, he had seized the land, he had turned off its guardian, and now, in a wild whirlwind, the results of his misdoing were upon him. He did not look at Tom Brighton's set face but at Jasper Peyton, the one he had wronged most.

"A man can't live without friends," he said. "Will you stand by me, Jasper, not for what I deserve, but for what I need?"

"Yes," answered Jasper Peyton. He smiled suddenly, with all the old, tense misery quite gone from his face. "We're going to stand by you, Anthony, all of us. We are with you still."

CHAPTER XII.

MEDFORD RIVER

Cousin Tom was giving rapid directions as they went out to the waiting automobiles. "I will go on with Jasper and we will pick up some men from the farms as we pass. Anthony, you had better come with Oliver, we shall want to crowd in all the farmers we can. What is it, Polly? You want to come with me? I suspect you think you are going to keep your father out of danger and I think the same of you. There is room in front here, between us; jump in!"

The engine grumbled and roared and the first car slid away into the shadows.

"Get in," said Oliver curtly to Anthony Crawford, while Janet opened the door of the second motor and slipped to the far side to give him room. None of the three spoke as they went down the drive behind Cousin Tom. As they came through the gate they could hear, faintly, the wild clanging of the bell in the valley below.

Oliver was too much occupied with his driving to have any other thought, Janet was awed into silence by the alien presence at her side, but Anthony Crawford, in that same husky, broken voice, suddenly began to speak as though he were following his thoughts out loud.

"I don't know why I came back to Medford Valley," he said. "I had lived through every sort of thing since I went away, but I was making good at last. Martha—that's the girl I married, she was a miner's daughter—had helped me to go straight. I was working in a mine, harder work than I had ever dreamed of in my life. It was good for me, yet I kept telling myself that it was being in prison. Perhaps it was, but I had forgotten that prison was the place where I ought to be."

Oliver tilted back his head that he might hear better, but his only answer was an inarticulate sound like a mutter of agreement. To reach the valley as soon as possible and without mishap, was more important to him, at that moment, than explanations. But Janet looked up with round, wondering eyes, eager to hear the rest.

"I kept thinking how it was here at home, so green and clean and peaceful, not like that stark, bare mountain country where I seemed to be working my whole life away. I told myself that a certain portion of Medford Valley belonged to me, that I could come back and live a life of dignified idleness, if only I had my rights, if only Jasper would give me what was my own."

"But it wasn't true. You knew that he wouldn't keep what belonged to you," burst out Janet.

"I knew it wasn't true, but people love to deceive themselves, and I had to explain to Martha. She would never have come if she had known how things really stood; she was unwilling, even as it was. But I was so sure, I thought I knew Jasper so well, exactly how I could threaten him, just where I could hurt him most. Had I not learned, when I was a boy, how proud and sensitive and generous he could be? I was as successful as I had hoped to be, but I wanted more and more, and see where it has brought me in the end!"

It seemed a relief to him to confess the very whole of his wrong-doing, to leave hidden no single meanness or small-souled thought. It was as though, in the clean night air, in the face of two just and clear-seeing companions, he wished to cast aside all the wrong of the past before making a new beginning.

"I am going away," he said. "It isn't because I found that my plan didn't pay as I had hoped it would. It is because I was happier back there in the West, serving out a sentence at hard labor, learning to live by the work of my hands rather than by my dishonorable wits. I can look back over my life and see just where my honesty began to waver, just when I first compromised with my own conscience and persuaded myself that something was fair and honest when I knew it was not. We had all the same chance, Jasper and Tom and I; look at them and look at me. You may wonder why I say all this to you. Perhaps it is because you alone saw through me, dared to tell me that I had no confidence even in my own claims, called me a man of straw and a bogy. Well, after to-night I am going back, to be a real man again."

For the first time Oliver slackened the speed of the car and nearly stopped in the road.

"Do you want to go now?" he inquired shortly. "We can take you to the station if you do. They don't need us down there, as they do the others."

"No, not now. I must know what my criminal bungling has amounted to, first. When I have seen the flood go down, then it will be time to go. I want to see this thing through."

They had straightened out into the level road and were forced to drive more slowly, for the highway was no longer empty. A big tractor was lumbering ahead, farm wagons turned out for them to pass, and hastily dressed men were thronging alongside. Two of them jumped upon the running board, but, seeing who sat in the car, muttered some imprecation and dropped off again. Anthony Crawford stood up and opened the door.

"I'll walk," he announced briefly. "Load in all the men you can carry. You will need every one."

Janet climbed over to the place beside her brother, and the tonneau filled up with men, who crowded the seats, clung to the step and the fenders, and sat in a row across the back of the car. They came to the end of the road at last where, in that place that had been so empty and quiet half an hour ago, there was now gathered a surging crowd of men, of horses, tractors, automobiles, and wagons. Oliver could see, on a knoll above the others, Polly standing with two farmers' wives, the only women there.

At first he could not see the water, but, as they pressed into the crowd, he caught sight of the broad pool, dark even in the moonlight. It was over the road, now, through the fence, and had crept halfway across the stretch of grass before John Massey's door. Tom Brighton's white-clad figure was going back and forth among the men, but it was Cousin Jasper, standing high above the others on the seat of a wagon, who was directing operations and getting this confused army of workers into rapid organization.

"Tom, take half the men to shovel dirt and pile up the sand sacks, and send the other half back to the sand pits to fill them. Clear the road so that the wagons can go back and forth. Henry Brook, take out your horses and join your team with Johnson's, the tractor can pull two wagons and we need four horses to each of the others. Now, go to it and bring the sandbags as fast as they can be filled. We can't save John Massey's house, but we will build a dam to hold the water a hundred yards back, where the ground begins to rise. And remember, you can't be too quick if you want to save the valley."

Oliver took off his coat and jumped out of the car.

"Go over where Polly is," he told Janet "I am going into this game with the others."

He was in every portion of it, as the night wore by, never quite knowing how he passed from one task to another, but following orders blindly, hour after hour. He helped to dig, but was not quite so quick as the others; he carried the sacks of sand that were brought up, loaded high upon the wagons, but he had not the quick swing of the more sturdy farmers.

The Windy Hill

He found himself at last on the high, vibrating seat of the heavy tractor, rumbling down the road with a line of wagons behind him, stopping at the sand pits to have them filled, then turning laboriously to haul them back again. The owner sat beside him on the first trip, directing him how to manage the unfamiliar machine, but as they made ready for a second he ejaculated, "You'll do," and jumped down to labor with the diggers. Oliver was left to drive his clumsy, powerful steed alone.

He saw the broad, semicircular wall of piled sandbags, banked with earth, rise slowly as the men worked with feverish haste, he saw the water come up to the foot of it, seem to hesitate, and then creep up the side. He saw, suddenly, just as they had all stopped to breathe, a long portion of the dike begin to tremble, then cave in with a hideous, sucking crash that shook the ground under them, he saw the flood of muddy water come roaring in and sweep against the painfully built rampart which swayed and crumbled to its fall.

In a wild turmoil of running, shouting men, backing wagons and rearing horses, he managed to extricate the clumsy monster that had been put under his care, brought it laboring and snorting out on higher ground and fell to work again. The barrier they had set up with so much toil was tumbling and collapsing in great gaps where the hungry current flung against it, but it held just long enough for them to raise another wall, longer, higher, firmer than the other and built with the frantic haste of desperate men.

The hours went by, it was long after midnight, with the sky growing pale for the morning. Once or twice Oliver had seen Anthony Crawford working among the rest, carrying sacks of sand, jostled and cursed by the men about him, but in spite of their abuse, toiling steadily onward. When the dike collapsed and the men ran for their lives, one wagon lurched off the road; its driver was flung from the seat and caught under the wheel, while the horses, having jammed the tongue against the bank, reared and plunged helplessly. Oliver saw Anthony Crawford run out, with the swift, muddy water flowing knee-deep around him, watched him extricate the man, drag him to the seat, and back the frantic horses away from the bank to bring them struggling through the water to safety. There was no time for words of commendation. Both men at once went back to their task of carrying sacks as the slow building of another wall began.

Some one had built a fire on the knoll, and here the farmers' wives, with Janet and Polly among them, were boiling coffee, frying bacon, and serving out food to the hungry, worn-out men. Oliver had munched a generous sandwich as he drove down the road. As he came back again he noticed a strange lull and observed that the men were leaning on their shovels and that the work had ceased. Tom Brighton, wet and muddy from head to foot, motioned him to come near.

"We've done all we can," the big farmer beside them was saying, "the sacks are nearly gone and the men are dead beat. If she breaks through now, the whole valley will have to go under."

The water was halfway up the side of the earth-banked wall and was still rising. Here and there a muddy trickle came oozing through, to be stopped by a clod of earth, but otherwise there was nothing to do. To Oliver it seemed that they stood for hours, staring, waiting as the water lifted slowly, rose half an inch, paused and rose again. It was three-fourths of the way up; it was a foot below the lip of the wall. The space of a foot dwindled to six inches.

"If there should be a wind, now," said the man beside him hoarsely.

Oliver looked back along the valley at the arch of sky showing blue instead of gray, at the trees moving gently in a morning breeze that touched the hilltop, but that did not stir the still air below. He heard Tom Brighton suddenly draw a sharp breath and he looked back quickly. Was

The Windy Hill

that space above the water a little wider, was there a wet black line that stretched all along the rough wall where the flood had touched and fallen again? He was not dreaming; it was true. The level of the muddy tide was dropping, the crest of the flood had passed.

It was broad daylight now, with the morning sunlight moving slowly down the slope into the valley. For the first time Oliver could see clearly the sullen, yellow pool of water, the crevasse in the dike, and John Massey's little house, submerged to its very eaves. He watched the shining streak of wet earth that marked the drop in the water, he saw it broaden into a ribbon and from a ribbon turn into a wide, glistening zone of safety that proved to all the danger had gone by.

"We can go now," said Cousin Tom at last. "There is work enough still to do, but it is time for us all to rest a little. We are certainly a wet and weary-looking crew."

They had breakfast, all of the cousins together, at Cousin Jasper's house, where Mrs. Brown, having spent half the night wringing her hands in helpless anxiety, had seemed to spend the other half superintending the preparation of a feast that should be truly worthy of the occasion. The guests were all cheerful and were still so keyed up by the struggle of the night that they did not yet feel weariness. Anthony Crawford sat on one side of Cousin Jasper, Tom Brighton on the other, while the three younger members of the party watched them wonderingly from the other end of the table. Everything, for the moment, seemed forgotten except the old comradeship of their boyhood. The only reminder of the unhappy days just passed lay in the atmosphere of relief and peacefulness that seemed to pervade the whole house.

The windows stood wide open and the morning wind came in to lift the long curtains and to stir the great bowl of flowers on the table. Oliver, hungrily devouring chicken and rolls and bacon and sausages and hot waffles with maple sirup, was saying little but was listening earnestly to the jokes and laughter of Cousin Jasper. After a day and night of anxiety, depression, struggle, and victory, he seemed suddenly to have become a new man. They were talking, the three elders, of their early adventures together, but Oliver noticed that the reminiscences never traveled beyond a certain year, that their stories would go forward to the time when they were nearly grown, and then would slip back to their younger days again. Some black memory was laid across the happy recollection of their friendship, cutting off all that came after; yet they talked and laughed easily of the bright, remote happiness that was common to them all. The boy noticed, also, as they sat together, that Anthony was like the others in certain ways, that his eyes could light with the same merriment as Cousin Jasper's, and that his chin was cut in the same determined line as Tom Brighton's. Yet—no—there was something about his face that never could be quite like theirs.

They had finished at last, and Anthony Crawford, pushing back his chair, came abruptly out of the past into the present. He thrust his hand into the inner pocket of his coat and brought out some legal-looking papers like those that Cousin Tom had locked away in the tin box.

"Here is the deed that you made out, Jasper, for the house and the land that you gave up to me. I put it in my pocket yesterday morning; it seems a year ago. The purpose I had then is something that I would rather forget, if I ever can. But this is what I do with it now."

He tore the heavy paper into pieces, smaller and smaller, as though he could not demolish completely enough the record of what he had demanded. The breeze from the garden sent the scraps fluttering over the table and across the rug, it carried the round, red seal along the tablecloth and dropped it into Janet's lap.

The Windy Hill

"Tom will have to make out some official papers," he said, "but I want you to understand this fully, that there among those fragments lies the end of this whole affair."

Cousin Jasper was about to speak, but Tom Brighton broke in ahead of him.

"It has turned out better than we could have hoped, Anthony," he began, "so that we can all agree to let bygones be bygones."

Anthony Crawford turned very slowly and looked, with those penetrating gray eyes, at Oliver.

"We owe a great deal to these children here," he said, "and as for one of them——"

Convinced that something was about to be said of him, Oliver got up quickly, pretending that it was merely because he had finished his breakfast and wished to be excused, hurried across the room, and slipped out through one of the long windows that opened on the terrace. He could still hear Anthony Crawford's voice, however, in the room behind him saying:

"It was these children who found the leak in the dike; it was Oliver who thought of going to look for it. It was Oliver who saw through me, saw that I had not a shred of honor or honesty behind my claim and told me what I was."

The boy moved farther away from the window so that he could not hear and stood, his hands clenched on the terrace rail, looking out over the garden, across the pools of color and stretches of green lawn, over the wall and down the white road that led away the length of the valley. No matter what words they might speak of him they could never make him forget how he had walked away down that road, meaning to leave all this vaguely understood trouble behind him. Only a chance meeting, the Beeman's friendly smile, the interest of a story that had caught him for a moment, and all would have been changed. No, there should be no words of praise for him.

153

The voices were louder behind him, for the three men were passing through the library, and Cousin Jasper was speaking just within.

"We still have to talk over this matter of rebuilding the dike," he said. "We must have your advice in that, Anthony."

"Go into the study," Anthony Crawford replied. "I must speak to Oliver for a moment."

He came out through the window while the others walked on together. Oliver turned to face him.

"I am going now," Anthony said quietly. "I thought you would be ready to help me when it was time."

Oliver reddened when he remembered the promptness of his offer the evening before.

"Do you need to go," he said awkwardly, "when you are friends again with every one here? Even the men in the valley don't hate you," he added bluntly, "after what you did last night. I believe Cousin Jasper will want you to stay."

"If I let him tell me so, I will not go," the other replied quickly. "It must be this minute, while my mind is still made up, or never. I will write to Martha to follow, I cannot even trust myself to wait for her. It is better that I should go, better for them, in the study there, better for the community, for myself, even better for you, Oliver, I know. Come," he insisted, as the boy still hesitated, "my confidence in you will be less great if you do not tell me that you know it also."

"Yes," returned Oliver grudgingly at last. "Yes, I know it too."

They drove away down the rain-washed, empty road with the early morning wind rushing about their ears. As they climbed to the highest ridge, Anthony Crawford stood up to look back down the sun-filled, green length of Medford Valley. Yet he did not speak until they had reached the station, with the train thundering in just as they drew up beside the platform.

The Windy Hill

"Good-by, Oliver," he said briefly.

The boy knew that the word of farewell was not for him but for all that the man was leaving—friends, memories, the place that he had loved in his strange, crooked way, all that he was putting behind him forever. A bell rang, a voice shouted the unintelligible something that stands for "All aboard," the train ground into motion, and he was gone.

Almost every one in Medford Valley must have slept that morning through the long hours until far past noon. But by four o'clock Oliver had slumbered all his weariness away, and so had Janet. They were restless after their excitement of the night before, and they found the house very still and with Cousin Jasper nowhere visible. They went out to the garage, got into the car, and set off along the familiar way toward the Windy Hill.

"Just to see if they are there," as Oliver said to Janet.

They came up the slope through the grass and saw the blue wood smoke rising lazily above them, unmistakable signal that the Beeman was at work. Polly greeted them gayly, for she, like them, was quite refreshed by the hours of slumber that had passed. Her father still looked weary, as though he had spent the interval in troubled thought rather than sleep, but he hailed them cheerily. All up and down the hill was a subdued and busy humming, for the day after rain is the best of all seasons for bees to gather honey.

"We thought we must find out what the storm had done to our hives," the Beeman said. "Only three were blown over, but there must have been a great commotion. Now we have everything set to rights and we are not in the mood, to tell the truth, for a great deal more work to-day."

"Are you too tired," Janet asked, "for—for a story?"

"No," he answered, "stories come easily for a man who has had training as Polly's father. I thought there was no one like her for demanding stories, but you are just such another."

They sat down on the grass with the broad shadow of the oak tree lying all about them and stretching farther and farther as the afternoon sun moved down the sky. They had chosen the steeper slope of the hill so that they could look down upon the whole length of the winding stream, the scattered house-tops, and the wide green of those gardenlike stretches that still lay, safe and serene, ripening their grain beside the river. The Beeman's eyes moved up and down the valley, resting longest upon the slope opposite, where the yellow farmhouse stood at the edge of its grove of trees and showed its wide gray roof, its white thread of pathway leading up to the door, its row of broad windows that were beginning to flash and shine under the touch of the level rays of the sun.

"Poor Anthony," he said slowly at last, "to be banished from a place he loved so much. And yet a person thinks it a little thing when he first confuses right with wrong!"

He drew a long breath and then turned to the girls with his old cheery smile.

"A story?" he repeated. "It will not be like the others, a tale from old dusty chronicles of Medford Valley, to tell you things that you should know. We have lived the last chapter of that tale and now we will go on to something new."

Oliver leaned back luxuriously in the grass, to stare up at the clear sky and the dark outline of the oak tree, clear-cut against the blue. Its heavy branches were just stirring in the unfailing breeze that blew in from the sea, and its rustling mingled sleepily with the Beeman's voice as he began:

"Once upon a time——"

Printed in the USA
CPSIA information can be obtained
at www.ICGtesting.com
LVHW051919020624
782068LV00004B/261